Isolina

Also by Dacia Maraini

The Silent Duchess

DACIA MARAINI

Isolina

Translated from the Italian by
Siân Williams

PETER OWEN

London & Chester Springs PA

PETER OWEN PUBLISHERS
73 Kenway Road London SW5 0RE
Peter Owen books are distributed in the USA by
Dufour Editions Inc. Chester Springs PA 19425–0449

First published in Italy by Mondadori 1985
© RCS Rizzoli Libri S.p.A., Milano 1992
First published in Great Britain 1993
English translation © Siân Williams 1993

The endpapers are based on *Study of a Young Girl* by Frederick Bridgman
(*courtesy of National Museum of American Art, Smithsonian Institution,
Washington DC*)

A catalogue record for this book is available from the British Library

ISBN 0–7206–0897–X

Printed and bound in Great Britain

Contents

Acknowledgements

I would like to thank the following: Pippo and Emanuela Zappulla, who helped me with my research in Verona on Isolina and Trivulzio; Paola Raguzzi, who collaborated with me in researching newspapers of the period and who suggested the idea of this trial to me; the lawyer, Guariente Guarienti, who accompanied me to the archives of the courts, made suggestions and clarified legal questions; Lucia di Stefano, who undertook research for me on Trivulzio and his family in Udine; Doctor Laura Castellazzo, who received me courteously at the State Archive; and Doctor Sebastiano Livoti, presiding judge at the court of Verona, who helped me with my search for the records of the Preliminary Investigation even though we unfortunately never found them.

PART ONE

The Facts

I

Verona. 16 January 1900. Two washerwomen were bent over, soaping sheets in the riverbed of the Adige just under the Garibaldi bridge.

From photographs of the time we can reconstruct how the river must have looked then: muddy, turbulent, just held back by its new banks (the Adige overflowed in 1882, destroying half the city); animated by the continual passage of boats carrying sand, barges with wide, brown sails, ferries that would go back and forth from one side to the other. Where the water ran more deeply and swiftly, floating water mills emerged, turning their dirty dripping paddles with a noisy creaking.

Along the banks, whether the day were fine or not, on the strips of stony beach there were lines of well-wrapped-up women, bent over their washing, chattering cheerfully amongst themselves.

Today the Garibaldi Bridge roots its granite arches in the pale water. A wall supports the pavement of the embankment on top of which cars run. Along the brick wall you can still see traces of the steps where the washerwomen would go down to the river.

It was at this point, where the water accumulates bits of plastic, old milk cans, and rags, that the washerwoman Maria Menapace, on the morning of 16 January 1900, saw a bag caught up in the undergrowth.

She showed it to her friend Luigia Marconcini saying, as she would later be quoted in the evidence, 'It must be cheap meat, someone's trying to avoid the tax on it.'

Not far off there was a boy fishing. He was bundled up in a black jerkin, a threadbare cap on his head, and a pair of patched ankle boots made of canvas. His name was Paride Baggio. He was fifteen. Menapace asked him to help her drag the bag to the bank.

The river police later described it as a 'voluminous bundle tied up with string'. 'That has to be something being smuggled in' they heard someone say from the bank. The two women left their washing to open it. The boy took out a knife with a wooden handle. He cut the string. Four curious hands unwrapped the cloth. And there they found 'six pieces of human flesh weighing 13,400 kg' as *L'Adige* reported next day.

The pieces were identified as 'the right side of the thorax with the whole breast wrapped up in a piece of scarlet cloth. The left side of the thorax with the breast wrapped up in the same kind of material. The lower part of the stomach wrapped up in green material of the same shade. A piece of the pelvic bone, from which the flesh had been stripped, wrapped up in the same green material. Part of the left leg wrapped up in a table-cloth. The thighbone, from which the flesh had been stripped, wrapped up in a pair of women's pants trimmed with lace'.

One detail was noted: a corner of the tablecloth was cut off as if to destroy a mark by which it might be recognized.

At twelve o'clock the Royal Prosecutor made his written report. The next day sappers from the 4th Genio regiment began to drag the river. In a few hours other pieces of the woman's body were retrieved: two bundles containing the intestines and another with the oesophagus, a placenta with the umbilical cord still attached to it.

When the pieces were put together, the experts established that it was the body of a young woman (aged between 16 and 22) who had an obvious curvature of the spine and was about three months pregnant. On the stage of the pregnancy there were to be conflicting opinions and endless discussions.

The whole city was alarmed. All of Verona was gripped by this crime. The hunt for the murderer began. Many people went to drag the river to try to find the head, which had not yet been retrieved.

On 17 January a miller found another piece: a hipbone wrapped up in a piece of skirt. In the folds of the skirt, hidden in a pocket, was a shopping list. The handwriting was shaky, rough and childish; it covered a piece of squared paper from an exercise book: 'Trousers for papa: 15 lire. Socks: 0.30 lira. Muslin and flannel: 8.35 lire. Red wool: 1.50 lire. Total: 25.15 lire.'

The chief constable, Cavalier Cacciatori, who was conducting the preliminary enquiries, asked about various girls who had disappeared. In the registers it appeared that on 5 January a certain Felice Canuti had reported the disappearance of his daughter, Isolina. They sent for him and showed him the list. The man recognized his daughter's handwriting.

Felice Canuti, whom the *Corriere della Sera* described as 'a stooped old man who moves slowly, with long white hair and beard, a long hooked nose, large sunken eyes, high cheekbones, thin, wearing threadbare clothes', was sixty-one and spoke very lovingly about his daughter Isolina: 'She was my idol', he said, 'I lived for her glance'; 'I can't take it in that she's dead . . . she went away the morning of the 5th and hasn't been back since. . . .'

'And where was she going?'

'I don't know . . . my daughter Clelia saw her walking in the direction of the Officers' Club and the gasometer.'

'Do you recognize these clothes?'

'I think so. But ask Maria Policante. They were close friends. She would know better than me.'

The chief constable sent for Maria Policante and interrogated her for a long time. Unfortunately, no trace of these interrogations remains, either in the State Archive, or in the Court, or in the Library of Verona. Everything was destroyed. Accidentally? Deliberately?

What do remain and can be studied are the articles in the newspapers of the time, *Il Gazzettino di Venezia, Corriere della Sera, L'Arena, L'Adige, Verona del Popolo, Verona Fedele, L'Italia Militare, Resto del Carlino, La Stampa.* Dailies, which as the investigation went on became mortal enemies divided into two opposing camps: the innocent and the guilty.

The name Carlo Trivulzio immediately stood out amongst

those who were first suspected. He was a lieutenant in the Alpini regiment who had rented a room at the Canutis' house and had had a relationship with Isolina. Trivulzio belonged to a noble family from Udine, was rich, and was respected and liked by his army comrades and superiors. 'A loyal, courageous, sincere young man incapable of such an horrendous deed' was the opinion most widely expressed by the army.

A few days later they arrived at a definite identification of the girl found cut up in pieces. All the Italian newspapers ran the story. She was Isolina Canuti, aged nineteen, daughter of Felice Canuti and Nerina Spinelli. Her father had been employed for the past twenty-five years as manager of a large business, Tressa of Verona.

Isolina had three siblings. Viscardo aged twelve, Alfredo aged thirteen, and Clelia aged sixteen. The mother had died more than ten years ago. The children lived alone with their father.

A theory was put forward that there had been an unsuccessful abortion and that the body had been quartered in order to destroy all traces of it. The experts all agreed in their reports that the cutting up was done by an 'expert hand', either that 'of a surgeon or a butcher'.

'A morbid interest in the crime has developed in Verona. The city talks about nothing else and crowds line the Adige in the hope of seeing some bloody bundle emerge.'

Someone adopting the role of moralist in the *Gazzetta di Treviso* wondered whether this was 'a legitimate feeling of curiosity or if this search for horror is a rather less comforting indication of neurotic excitability and therefore of a mental and physical decadence'.

II

On 22 January the newspapers published some unexpected news: Lieutenant Trivulzio and a midwife named Friedman had been arrested. There were rumours of the interrogation of these two suspects in unconfirmed reports by the press. Trivulzio admitted having been Isolina's lover, even if only for a short time. He admitted knowing Isolina was pregnant but denied having urged her to have an abortion. He denied ever having gone out with Isolina even though there were two witnesses (a priest and an innkeeper) who saw them together at the Chiodo, that same trattoria where they said the girl was killed. Trivulzio denied having had anything to do with the girl in the period dating from her disappearance until her remains were found.

The midwife Friedman, whom it seems Isolina had been to see with her friend Maria Policante, denied everything, admitting only that she knew Isolina and that she had once put Maria Policante up as a guest.

The main accusations against the lieutenant came from Isolina's younger sister, Clelia Canuti, who was sixteen. Clelia said that at an open door she heard Trivulzio asking her sister if she had taken the powder to induce an abortion, for which he had given her the money.

Isolina had replied: 'I took the powder, but nothing happened.' He then said, 'In no circumstances do I want you to have the baby in Verona; either have an abortion here or else I shall send you to Milan.'

Maria Policante was also interrogated. She had been a servant at the Canutis' house but she left because they did not pay her regularly. But that was her story, because Felice Canuti said that he sent her away for setting a bad example to his daughter. In any event, she and Isolina were very close friends, and when Maria had an abortion – carried out by Friedman – Isolina would go every day to take her something to eat.

Maria Policante confirmed what Clelia said. Yes, Isolina was pregnant by Trivulzio but didn't want to have an abortion. The lieutenant had given her some money to buy a powder to bring on an abortion but she didn't take it; instead she pretended to and substituted another medicine which the doctor had prescribed her for rickets.

She also heard Trivulzio utter the famous remark to Isolina about Milan. The lieutenant did not want the girl to have a baby and was also prepared to spend some money to rid himself of the 'nuisance'.

'The lieutenant', wrote the *Corriere della Sera*, 'is twenty-five years old and belongs to the 6th regiment of the Alpini. He was arrested at 3.30 a.m. at 25 Via Cavour, the house where Isolina Canuti also lived. The lieutenant leads a sociable life, and that same night had been out in civilian clothes with some friends until 2 a.m. at a masked ball at the Ristori Theatre.'

The *Corriere della Sera* described Friedman, 'Born in Milan. Her face is disfigured by a terrible scar which deforms the lower part of it and leaves her teeth protruding. Friedman has been a midwife for nineteen years. She has already had trouble with the law on the two occasions when she abandoned a new-born baby on the steps of the orphanage. She knew Isolina Canuti two years ago when she took in the Canutis' domestic servant, Maria Policante. She adds that she stopped seeing Isolina because she had a "filthy mouth". Since then she hadn't seen her until last October.'

The newspapers, especially those in favour of Trivulzio, began to spread rumours that Isolina's behaviour 'was not beyond reproach'. They wrote about her as being a 'girl who was impatient with her father's restrictions', who 'would return home late at night', who 'had girlfriends and men friends with whom she would go out to dinner and have a good time', that 'lately she used to sleep in the sitting room with her sister Clelia'.

According to Clelia, 'Isolina wanted to keep the baby, but Trivulzio didn't.' 'The child of a hunchback who's had rickets, like her?' said the lieutenant. 'No, never.'

'Tall, with a pleasant personality, Carlo Trivulzio left school in Modena in 1894, and went first into the army as a sergeant in the 4th Division of the Fanteria and then as sub-lieutenant in the 6th Division of the Alpini. He was made a lieutenant in 1898. When he returned from Bassano he went to live in Felice Canuti's house where he had intimate relations with Isolina, an unattractive girl, whose morals left something to be desired. . . .'

'The father, a widower for the last ten years, who was away at work the whole day, needed Isolina to be a mother to the younger children. Instead, the girl, as the neighbours also confirm, had a good time and took little interest in her domestic duties. The consequences of such behaviour were not slow to manifest themselves. The neighbours mutter that Isolina had to go to Friedman on more than one occasion.'

Meanwhile, Trivulzio protested his innocence from the Scalzi Prison. He swore that on the night the crime was committed he was on picket-duty.

People wondered – but where was Isolina from 5 January until the day of the crime? Where did she die? Where was she cut up? Why did the murderers throw the pieces in the Adige and leave a compromising list in the pocket instead of burying everything as they presumably did with the head?

The journalists meanwhile ran riot. Apart from *L'Adige* and other local dailies which asked for privileges for the officers, the *Corriere della Sera* and *Il Gazzettino* carried out parallel enquiries and sent journalists to the Canutis' house and Trivulzio's house in Udine.

'Towards evening our correspondent goes to find the Canuti family. An old woman opens the door and there are three young children sitting at the table. When she is questioned, the old woman, with tears in her eyes, asks one of the little ones to reply for her: "You talk – I don't have the heart."'

The children were Viscardo, Alfredo and Clelia. Alfredo said they were usually on their own because their father was working and their mother was dead. Their old aunt, Angela Spinelli, had arrived only a few hours ago. He said Isolina might have gone away on 5 January and had already gone away on other occasions for several days. 'When we asked those same children if they wished their sister well, all three replied, "No, because she used to upset Papa so much". Only Alfredo added "She understood that she'd always be our sister though!"'

Someone else went to question the family doctor. 'Isolina was anaemic,' the doctor told the correspondent, 'and she was scrofulous.' Almost two months earlier she had gone with her father to be treated for anaemia and he had prescribed an iron treatment but he had not realized she was pregnant. Had she been four months pregnant as was maintained, then he would have been aware of it. On the 7th the doctor again saw Felice Canuti who said to him: 'Something terrible has happened to me – my daughter Isolina has run away from home!'

Nor should her friend Maria Policante be forgotten. She stated: 'I heard Lieutenant Trivulzio say to Isolina that it wasn't such a terrible thing he was asking her to do, and that other girls had already done it for him and were well and happy. One day, when I interrupted to say what I thought, he told me that Isolina was a stubborn mule.'

'Young and charming', Lieutenant Trivulzio 'was always smiling, and a well-known client of the most elegant and lively meeting places in town. For those who know him he is certainly the last person to fall under suspicion for this horrible deed. Even last night he was carefree and happy – outwardly at least – at the early carnival festivities.'

The news of his arrest was a shock to everyone. 'It "was conveyed to his mother Signora Verzegnassi" with the utmost delicacy by an officer. She says that Carlo was to go on leave to Udine but his duties prevented him. Another son is also in the army.'

The *Gazzetta di Venezia* called for privileges for officers, regretting that there were not more of them. And it concluded: 'In addition, we are insistent that the process of gaining the lieutenant's freedom will soon be a *fait accompli*, in our firm belief that the authorities – such as they are – have made a grave and unjust mistake in imprisoning the person they think guilty. We hope that the government intends to give a severe lesson to those officials who are so pathetically incompetent.'

On 27 January the mayor paid a visit to the commander of the 6th Division of the Alpini to assure him that the events in progress had in no way 'changed the attitude of the people towards the army in general and the Alpini in particular'.

III

The newspaper *Verona del Popolo*, was the first to write that according to definite evidence, the crime was committed in a restaurant, the Chiodo, in Vicolo Chiodo, during an officers' dinner. And that the midwife Friedman had had nothing to do with what had happened.

Meanwhile, Trivulzio wrote a letter to his colonel from prison:

> My dear colonel, forgive me for taking the liberty of writing to you, but you are now like a second father to me. Yesterday I cried with gratitude when I learned that you had immediately thought about my mother: only I can appreciate the delicacy of your action. I cried bitter tears thinking about the pain which all those who love me and whom I love must have suffered, but I comfort myself with the knowledge that not one of them would ever believe that I could be a criminal. I swear to you colonel, that were I the person guilty I would already have killed myself. But I need to live and the honour of my name and my regiment demand it.
>
> I must show everyone that I am as honourable as before and that if fatal circumstances have implicated me in a crime, I swear that there is nothing, nothing that torments my conscience. But first I have to disentangle myself from a web of inexplicable evidence which is working against me. With God's help, I shall certainly be cleared, because truth will always win out sooner or later. Meanwhile, I beg you to let my colleagues know that I feel something much stronger than gratitude for their not losing faith in me, and for what they have done for me and my mother. She is old. It is a blow that could kill her. God does not wish this. For this reason and no other, I shed tears. All the rest I can face calmly. At this moment Lieutenant Moratti [who went to Udine to take the sad news to his mother] will be there with her. Perhaps even now she already knows. May God help me! Colonel, I entrust her to your care. Forgive me for asking so much of you like this. From your subordinate,

Carlo Trivulzio

And there was more:

P.S. Please be tolerant sir, of my hope of seeing you again
soon: I have faith in man's justice, but even more in God's.
This and a pure conscience is all I need.

The letter, which was published in *L'Arena*, stirred up posi-
tive feeling in the town. That same evening there was a demon-
stration in the Piazza Bra. The Alpini brass band 'is applauded
and accompanied right to the barracks with people cheering the
army and the Alpini'.

'A rumour is going round that a Veronese newspaper today
received an anonymous postcard postmarked Rouen, which said
that the woman cut up in pieces was a noblewoman from Geneva
and that the crime was committed in a cellar in Via Colomba
where even now the head and arms are still walled up. . . .'

'There's also talk of a telegram sent by Isolina and her lover to
her father, but this is definitely refuted by evening.'

The newspapers gossiped. Isolina became a national case.
Italy was divided in two: those who believed in a plot against
the army ('how could an officer possibly be implicated in such
filth, and after all, who was the victim? A slut, a prostitute! If
she put up with violence it means she wanted it! How could
you trust someone like her? Certainly it's someone else's child
and a plot to blacken the 6th Division of the Alpini by means of
one of its most respected officers! Naturally the socialists will
make something of it to spread low anti-military propaganda –
it's a crying shame!'), and those people who on the contrary
thought that an horrendous injustice was being done ('a young
girl has been killed and cut up in pieces; all the clues point to
Trivulzio; the chief constable right at the beginning interrogated
him and arrested him, but then pressure came from higher
authorities – the President of the Cabinet, it's known, is a
military man – and already people talk about his release; only
the socialists are keeping the case going by accusing Trivulzio,
even if he is not actually guilty himself, of being implicated in
the murder and the disposal of the body').

In all this a morbid attention was concentrated on the figure
of Lieutenant Trivulzio.

'Every day in Scalzi Prison the lieutenant receives food from outside. He gets up early in the morning and spends the day quietly reading books from the prison library.'

His mother, Signora Verzegnassi, to whom the news of the arrest of her son was conveyed with the utmost tact by an officer in civilian clothes, was in shock and inconsolable.

The socialist weekly, *Verona del Popolo*, ran a harsh rhetorical commentary. 'In the kind of society in which we exist, where it is understood that men see hunting women as a glorious sport, women have to contend with a legal system which is not of their making. So for example, if a woman succumbs to seduction and the consequence of her fall is a baby born outside the legal institution of marriage, she has to suffer stigma and shame. Men who are cowardly, however, in order to avoid this kind of dishonour – which, if it is a dishonour, should be atoned for by both parties – have recourse to crime, even murder, so that their reputation can remain untarnished.'

Then it addressed the women of Verona: 'Women of Verona, wives, mothers, daughters, sisters, who when reading *L'Arena* lately will have felt all the disgust that a soul can experience on being faced with the most infamous profanity which that newspaper spits on the unburied remains of poor Isolina Canuti, hear and do not forget, hear and commemorate. . . .'

'Praise to the worthy officials who, having discovered those guilty of quartering Isolina Canuti, were unable to imagine that they might be protected by the head of the same government that had promised a reward for pursuing the guilty with the utmost urgency. All, because it was firmly believed that not simply one person was guilty but that several people must have taken part in the crime.

'And yet an order, coming from the same source as the promised reward, silenced those who knew. After that order, one newspaper changed its tone. While it seemed the crime could be attributed to someone from the lower classes, the usual violent language was used by the newspaper, but once Lieutenant Trivulzio and other remotely possible murderers were arrested and the crime began to appear to be connected with the upper echelons of society, then from that point on, the newspaper began to sow doubts. . . .'

'It is a new Dreyfus Affair' the *Corriere della Sera* commented on 27 January. 'The fact is that until now no crushing proof has emerged against the suspects, not even a definite identification of the body.' The *Corriere della Sera* then adopted the same stance as *L'Adige*.

The military authorities confirmed that on the night of the 15th Carlo Trivulzio was on picket-duty. The police meanwhile confirmed the charge of 'premeditated murder' against Lieutenant Trivulzio.

The chief constable replied to questions put by a journalist, by saying that they had a body and that all the clues they had found pointed to Lieutenant Trivulzio. On this occasion, the chief constable complained about being pressured by the Ministry of the Interior to release the lieutenant.

'At 2 p.m. today (27 January 1900) the lieutenant met his brother again in Scalzi Prison and asked him to look after their mother.'

The military newspaper *La Sentinella* published another letter from Carlo Trivulzio to a solicitor friend, Cantu di Brescia, who had spontaneously offered to defend him.

Dear Mario, In difficult circumstances we recognize who our friends are. Your voice, until now silent for seven years, speaks out when misfortune befalls me. It is unnecessary for me to protest my innocence to you. I only want to thank you from the bottom of my heart. I hope that I shall not need your kind offer because I am undergoing a preliminary investigation which should make things sufficiently clear; only if I need to shall I ask you for help, in the form of your knowledge, your eloquence, your loyalty and your friendship. A heartfelt goodbye, and a kiss from your Carlo.

The solicitor Cantu did not, however, defend Trivulzio in the Todeschini trial.

IV

On the 6th and 7th the suspects were interrogated again. 'As there is no overwhelming evidence against the two of them, the examining judge guarantees that on the 10th he will announce that they can be released.' Instead, the two were let out that same evening, the 7th, on a temporary basis. The chief constable made a public announcement that 'all the reasons to suspect Trivulzio still exist . . .', that 'we are in no doubt, no matter what the newspapers say, that it is Isolina's body, because in addition to the clothes recognized by both her father and sister and also the shopping list, no other girl disappeared at that time and the ones who were supposed to have disappeared turned up again. The investigations continue.'

Details of Trivulzio's release: 'As soon as he was released Trivulzio went immediately to the barracks to Colonel Comi's quarters, threw his arms around his neck and the colonel even kissed and hugged him, insisting that he stay for dinner. . . .'

'But the lieutenant preferred to leave immediately for Udine where his mother was waiting for him.'

'A group of his friends stopped him on the road and made him postpone his departure in order to go to the Chiodo to congratulate him. The young officer was visibly moved when the Chiodo song resounded triumphantly to the sound of clinking glasses.' This was reported in *L'Arena* on 9 February 1900.

The journalist went to find the midwife Friedman. 'Are you thinking of continuing to work as a midwife after this disaster?' The woman, lifting up her ugly face deformed by a scar, replied, 'Yes, because my conscience is clear. That's if I can find more work, because this arrest has done my reputation a lot of damage.'

There immediately followed an interview with the lieutenant who had just been released. The *Corriere della Sera* on 10.2.1900 asked: 'How does Lieutenant Trivulzio explain his arrest?' The handsome young man, calm and smiling, replied, 'It was an accumulation of the most trivial circumstances which the authorities, in making out a case, believed that they could make seem worse than they actually were: my living with Isolina, our rooms being on the same landing, her visits to my room, my

going out at night in civilian clothes, my help with her pregnancy, her fear of her father etc. . . .'

'"Were you affected by the arrest?"

'"Yes, it made me very unhappy thinking about my mother
and the honour of my family. However, I was very calm because I believed that justice would be done. Even the warders
were amazed by it. My mother also wrote to me urging me to
keep calm. I suspected, though, that they were hiding her real
condition. . . ." When talking about his mother, the lieutenant
was almost moved to tears.'

The journalist pressed him, '"And the interrogations?"', and
the lieutenant replied: '"I underwent three interrogations but
I'm not able to talk about them freely. My relationship with
Isolina was very brief and an altogether occasional one. My
relationship with the Canuti family was always excellent, even
at the end when I tried to comfort her father who poured out all
his feelings to me. When I was arrested I was always sure that
justice would be done. The judges and the State Prosecutor
were always available to me. I am sorry to learn that my case
has been used as a pretext for a controversy that confuses me
with the institution to which I belong. It is an institution to
which I am entitled to belong and in which I take pride.

'When I was in prison, I received expressions of solidarity
from all over Italy, even from strangers. After I was released,
the letters and telegrams multiplied. The comradeship of my
companions, the goodness and the delicacy of the colonel were
a great comfort and consolation to my mother."

'"But you have only been granted a conditional freedom? So
you are still under suspicion."

'"I would have preferred to be released unconditionally, but
the judge reassured me that I would be acquitted. Because of
this I accepted, otherwise I would not have been able to go and
see my dearest mother."

'"But someone claimed that the body is not Isolina's. Was it
you?"

'"They say that the clothes have been recognized by her
relatives, but I still have some doubts as to whether it really is
her body. Why are the clothes considered evidence?"'

Here Trivulzio made a psychological mistake. His stubborn refusal to recognize the body when everyone had confirmed that it was Isolina's was indicative of an obviously extreme desire to deflect suspicion from himself in the simplest way possible, by denying the evidence.

The journalist continued to press him with questions.

'"Do you bear any grudges towards anyone?"'

'"No, I don't have a grudge against anyone,"' Trivulzio replied arrogantly. '"I feel reassured and confident that justice will be done."'

Meanwhile, *L'Adige* reported some news from *Il Gazzettino* about evidence given by some people who maintained that they saw Isolina go into the Chiodo on the night of 5 January.

The fact is that the public was so avid for news that the newspaper had to report the least trifle. Even if it then went on to tear it to pieces by discrediting the witnesses and reiterating its firm conviction: Trivulzio is innocent.

And so both the *Corriere della Sera* and *L'Adige*, probably in order not to lose any readers at this point, rushed to report the most important news on Isolina's death.

'Yesterday the experts handed in their conclusions to the judicial authorities' wrote the *Corriere* on 11 February. 'From his examination of the mammary glands Professor Bonuzzi deduced that Isolina was four months pregnant.' (A year later, at Todeschini's trial, the same Bonuzzi would say that he was sure the girl was seven months pregnant.)

'The experts Pisa and Fagioli who examined all the other pieces, by multiplying the length of the femur by four, have calculated that the body that was found was about 1 m 60 cm in height. As for the bruises on the collar-bone, the doctors believe that these were made while the woman was alive. By now no one has any further doubts about the identity of the corpse.'

On 12 February, the *Corriere* returned to the experts' opinion on the bruises found on the collar-bone: 'The doctors are convinced that they must have been made while the woman was still alive and this, linked to the fact that all the pieces of flesh that have been found show internal bleeding, makes one believe that the woman suffered a violent death, either from suffocation or poisoning. . . . Poison is suspected in view of the fact that care has been taken to destroy all the intestines and to clean out the pelvis completely.

'From the way in which the body was cut up – especially the arms and the respective joints – it is evident that it was done by an expert.'

V

On 24 February, something very serious happened: one of Isolina's closest friends, Emma Poli, died. Emma had been with Isolina at the dinner at the Chiodo, as she herself revealed, and was also present at her friend's abortion.

She was to be interrogated by the judges. But 'the authorities were not able to see her given the gravity of her condition. The woman had just given birth without any difficulty. But after the birth, her condition worsened. She seemed to get better in the days following, and then yesterday she suddenly died.'

And so an essential witness who had been silent up to her death, either from fear or inertia, disappeared. But before she died, Emma Poli told her father that she had been poisoned.

Benedetto Poli, her father, went to the chief constable, but he would not see him. He spoke to a police officer and told him what he knew. The officer advised him not to take any notice of a dying person's last words; let her go in peace, this has nothing to do with the enquiry with which we are dealing.

Poli returned home. He wrote a letter to the chief constable. He reported the facts, brought up the names of two people, Ronconi and Zamboni, who might have been the ones responsible for his daughter's death. But no one sent for him.

Nothing was mentioned about these incidents until the opening of Todeschini's trial almost a year later.

An even more sinister fact . . . the director of the hospital where Emma Poli died was Doctor Bonuzzi who, using his medical expertise, did everything to support Trivulzio's innocence – even at the risk of contradicting himself as he did: in his expert opinion on the pregnancy he said first that it was four months, and then seven. And it was to be his medical expertise that decided the credibility of some witnesses. Of one he would say that the person concerned was incapable of 'understanding and reasoning', of another that he had 'a weak character' and was therefore suggestible and untrustworthy.

Everyone knew that Emma Poli was a decisive witness. The way in which she was said to have died was unconvincing. But at the same time, no one wanted to believe what her father said. Who said where Emma had been with Isolina on the evening of the crime? Poli, who heard it from his daughter. But who could believe him when he accused two highly respectable men – Zamboni, a famous lawyer, and Ronconi, a famous physician – of responsibility for his daughter's death?

No one would do anything to examine the business more fully. Not even the journalists. It was almost two years later that it was known that the Zamboni who had been accused by Poli had nothing to do with the crime. The fact was that because Emma had referred to him by his surname alone, and Verona is full of Zambonis, Benedetto Poli had chosen the most well known, thus making many people hate him and significantly reducing his credibility.

At the trial, Todeschini was to reveal that there was indeed a certain Zamboni, a soldier, who was being taken care of in hospital in exactly the same period in which Emma was recovering (evidence given by Doctor Storate on 24 November 1901). But by then it was too late. The whole Poli business had been buried in silence. And no one, not even the lawyers on the opposing side, would risk delving deeper.

VI

From March until October, the newspapers no longer wrote about Isolina. Like a big fire which needs fuel to keep it going, people's curiosity grew weak and was extinguished.

It seemed that everything was being resolved by silence and oblivion. Trivulzio had been reunited with his 'adored mamma' and was on holiday in Udine. The military was satisfied. Nothing was heard of the Canuti family. The silence of a city entering a torrid and desperate summer fell upon Isolina. Prices rose, people were homeless.

Few people could allow themselves a holiday. To compensate for this there were some wonderful new forms of entertainment: a strange gadget with a complicated name which projected seductive shadows onto a white screen; the Great Exhibition inaugurated by the Duke d'Aosta with oriental kiosks, flower competitions and open-air banquets.

It seemed that only Felice Canuti remembered his daughter, and tried to accustom himself to the idea of his loss. But he did nothing to resurrect the case, to discover who was guilty. His mistrust of the world and of justice was so great that he shut himself up at home and nursed an unrelieved anguish.

There are no portraits of Isolina. What do we know about her? 'Scorpion, little cow, monkey' Trivulzio called her. 'Anaemic, scrofulous' said the doctor. 'A short, hunchbacked, ugly thing' said the neighbours. Altogether a deformed creature devoid of attraction.

And yet Isolina knew how to enchant, had loyal friends and lovers so persistent that she got a reputation for being 'a loose, depraved slut' amongst the people in the neighbourhood.

The truth of the matter was that at nineteen, Isolina had had two lovers: the first a lieutenant in the Bersaglieri who was called Petrini, the second, Lieutenant Trivulzio, by whom she became pregnant.

We know that Isolina loved to dance, to go out at night, to be with friends and have young men court her. Her father said that she 'had the devil in her' and that must have been true, because everyone described her as affectionate, vivacious, impatient with any attempt to restrain her, curious and intelligent. From the few things we know about her we get a picture of a sweet person, childish, greedy for amusement but neither cynical nor malicious.

When her friend Maria Policante was in bed at the midwife Friedman's house after she had had an abortion, Isolina went there every day to take her something to eat.

Let us imagine her, with her long scarlet skirt, her light step taking her quickly towards the midwife's house with a bundle in her arms: a hot plate wrapped up in a bit of kitchen cloth, some bread just out of the oven, some aniseed biscuits, a half bottle of wine.

We know that she adored sweet mustard. The grocer Oreste Fiorio, who at the Todeschini trial was a witness against her, said that he sold her some sweet mustard on the same morning that she disappeared.

We know that she wanted to keep the baby despite the fact that she was poor and liked to have a good time. More than once she said to her sister and Trivulzio that she did not want to have an abortion. 'I'm keeping a little Alpino warm' she said to Clelia one day as she patted her stomach (evidence from the Todeschini trial).

And on another occasion, she said to her lover's orderly 'I've got a little Trivulzio in here.' And when Trivulzio was forcing her to have an abortion she said to Maria Policante, 'I'm waiting for him to take his holiday and then I shall rent a room and have the baby, and he will pay.'

From this and other things she said, we can guess that Isolina was in love with Trivulzio. She had ordered an embroidered bodice from the tailor Vianello (another witness against her) and she wore it when 'she went to bed with him' (Clelia's evidence).

Once she sold a ring which her mother had left her so that she could buy eggs and marsala in order to make 'zabaglione for my love'.

And she said to Zampieri, the laundryman who gave evidence against her at the Todeschini trial and said that her behaviour was scandalous, 'Washerman, washerman, my lover has left me. . . .'

Altogether an exuberant character then, joyful and restless. She did not care a great deal about money – when she had it, she spent it.

She dreamed, like all poor people, about expensive and beautiful things. She was very fond of her sister Clelia who was four years younger. She would tell her everything without missing a detail. Sometimes she excluded her when she was having a good time, and this provoked that envy which was heard in her little sister's words at the trial.

Isolina loved her father madly. But she treated him a bit like she treated her lovers: she was passionate about them, but it was a capricious passion, tinged with amusement.

VII

On 16 October *Il Gazzettino di Venezia* published a new name which had not been heard of until then: the midwife De Mori. It was revealed by various pieces of evidence. De Mori asserted that a woman went to see her on behalf of Lieutenant Trivulzio to ask her to perform an abortion on a young girl. She had even written his name on a wall. The journalist saw the name which was spelled incorrectly, Tribulzio instead of Trivulzio.

On the 19th the Honourable Monti was questioned in Parliament about the Canuti affair, which was going to be reopened because 'new facts have come to light which have changed the situation'.

The Honourable Balenzano replied to the Honourable Monti, stating that 'the preliminary investigation will be reopened following new facts which have emerged and that progress must be made regardless of anyone'.

On 19 October the Veronese socialist deputy, the Honourable Mario Todeschini, presented the Chamber with another written demand: 'The undersigned makes enquiries of the Ministers of Justice, the Ministers for Internal Affairs, and the Minister for Defence, about the local magistracy, and the military authorities regarding the crime of the woman who was cut up into pieces, specifically about negligence during the preliminary investigation, the investigations carried out by the police and by the military authorities.'

The next day they wrote in the *Corriere della Sera* that the Royal Prosecutor stated: 'It's impossible to reopen the trial against Lieutenant Trivulzio based on the new revelations published in *Il Gazzettino di Venezia* insofar as these were already known to the authorities at the end of last April, and they lack new facts necessary to be able to reopen the case.'

If they knew the facts, people asked, why ever didn't they mention them before? Why on earth was De Mori not interrogated, and why were she and Trivulzio not made to confront each other? The impression that both the public and the journalists gained from all this was that the authorities were keeping the whole business closed – or wanted to keep it closed.

The only ones not to give up were the socialists at *Verona del Popolo*. They, like other journalists, had been conducting their own private investigations and had found out things that were disconcerting, to say the least. They took a decision to get the trial reopened. In order to do this, they assumed the role of *provocateur*.

On 3 November the newspaper ran an editorial which challenged and attempted to flush out Trivulzio. The editors were obviously aiming for legal action to get the debate reopened.

'In the files of the examining judge are the following records: Clelia Canuti's testimony that she heard her sister say to Lieutenant Trivulzio, "I took the powder but nothing happened", to which the officer replied, "Whatever happens I don't want you to have a baby here in Verona; either have an abortion or I shall send you to Milan"; and secondly, De Mori's reply to the judge that she hadn't needed to lie because "no one ever questioned me about that". She was referring to the fact that Policante had given her the name of an officer – which sounded like Tribulzio – who was asking her to perform an abortion, and she had written it on a wall. Until all of this is proved to be untrue, we shall continue to maintain that the officer is a suspect, because however you look at it the authorities could take proceedings against him for trying to procure an abortion. It cannot be said, either, that the lieutenant's hands are tied by the official proceedings of the Council Chamber because the regulations are not irrevocable. In any case, it is always possible for him to be completely cleared simply by making an outright charge of

slander against De Mori, Policante, *Il Gazzettino*, or our newspaper.'

Verona del Popolo reported what had happened to Emma Poli.
'Her father, Benedetto Poli, reported to the authorities that
before she died, his daughter confided in him under oath that
she was not dying of puerperal fever, but poisoning. And
furthermore, she gave him the name of two gentlemen and said
that one of them had poisoned her so that she wouldn't tell the
truth about what happened to Isolina.

'Poli immediately reported everything to the police. Emma's
death took place on 20 February, the report was made on the
22nd, but a great deal of time passed before it was dealt with.
And yet no one thought to interrogate Poli or the two gentlemen who had been accused.'

A journalist from the *Corriere della Sera* went to find Poli. 'A
serious man, a worker, about fifty.' He asked if what they wrote
about him in *Verona* was true. 'He has no hesitation in confirm-
ing the news of his report.' He said that because of the oath
made by his daughter, he went to the authorities on 22 February, but the police paid no attention to what he reported. And
so he put it in writing, specifying further facts, on 20 June.
Nothing happened on that occasion either. He made a report
again on 7 July. But because the authorities continued to ignore
it, he repeatedly and publicly accused those he thought were
guilty. At the same time he began to prepare papers 'so as to get
a free defence for the criminal proceedings which he would
undertake against the two people whom his daughter had indi-
cated: Cavalier Pietro Zamboni and Cirillo Ronconi, two highly
respected people'.

Councillor Zamboni was highly indignant. He declared that
his brother had absolutely nothing to do with the crime: 'I don't
even know Emma Poli.' He talked about the pain his eighty-
year-old father was suffering and threatened to sue either Poli,
or the newspaper reporting the facts. He maintained that the
Royal Prosecutor had said to one of his friends, a lawyer, that
nothing had emerged against his brother.

There was no news of Trivulzio. He did not start proceedings. No one knew where he was. And Todeschini continued to

be provocative. On 20 October another article was published in
Verona del Popolo. '"We are not in a position to take proceedings
for Crime 383 [abortion carried out followed by death] because
if one looks hard at the evidence and proof collected in the
preliminary investigation, now closed, it cannot honestly be
said that Isolina Canuti's death appeared to be the result of a
crime." This is the stone that the Veronese Tribunal placed on
the unavenged remains of Isolina Canuti.'

Todeschini pursued his argument brilliantly, demonstrating
that given the evidence available, Trivulzio should be tried for
'trying to procure an abortion'. And if Isolina agreed to this, she
too, should be tried by default, given that the newspapers were
casting doubts on whether the body was actually hers.

He referred to conversations which would have taken place
between the Royal Prosecutor and the Police Superintendent 'in
relation to the mysterious crime which led to the butchering of
Isolina Canuti'.

'However, we are not satisfied that such meetings between
the two authorities could lead to the reopening of the proceedings. If by chance the will were there, there would be no need
for further talks.'

He remembered that the chief constable of Verona had talked
about 'a web in which the authorities examining the case were
entangled by someone who has an interest in keeping this
abominable crime in darkness', after which the chief constable
handed in his resignation. And Todeschini then directly
addressed the Minister of Defence and Internal Affairs, a Signor
Pelloux, asking him if 'in his capacity of Minister for Defence
and Internal Affairs he really had at his disposal a sum of 2000
lire as a reward for someone who could reveal the names of
those who cut up Isolina Canuti or whether he had in fact spent
a larger sum to keep those who knew quiet'.

And he continued: 'Naturally, no reply, no injunction or
proceedings against our newspaper which accused that same
Prime Minister of the crime of aiding and abetting.'

VIII

An important piece of news: the chief constable took back his resignation. And Todeschini commented in his newspaper: 'It is with a feeling of profound indignation that we note that even honest people do not know how to extricate themselves from contributing to hiding crimes such as the one in which Isolina Canuti lost her life.'

There was again no reply, and no proceedings were taken against either the newspaper or Todeschini.

So he continued, unperturbed. On 27 October he published another article in which he briefly retold the story of the crime for those who might have forgotten the facts. Almost a year had now passed since Isolina's death.

'After the bleak discovery of pieces of human flesh found on a bank of the Adige on 16 January, the press was unanimous in calling for maximum efforts to be made by the authorities, because it ought to be impossible for those guilty to avoid just punishment. And the police proved themselves to be so quick and efficient, that in a few days they were able to find out names and the circumstances of the crime. But when it was discovered that an officer in the Alpini regiment was implicated and that he had not acted alone, but in the company of other officers, suddenly that same government which had promised a reward to speed up a laborious hunt for those guilty, began to protect them by issuing orders for silence.

'Meanwhile, Lieutenant Trivulzio wrote a letter which appeared in the usual newspaper a few hours after it had been written. God in heaven, did they really want to fling mud at our glorious army, which has distinguished itself – even in our own city of Verona – during huge floods or earthquakes or fires, etc?

'At the same time the magistrate, pronouncing a sentence somewhere between no and yes, had the arrested lieutenant acquitted.'

Todeschini insisted that, from what he knew, Lieutenant Trivulzio should at the very least be accused of 'procuring an abortion'. He protested that the chief constable had never even heard what Policante had to say about the De Mori business. He asked why, if Trivulzio was so convinced that Clelia Canuti was telling lies he did not denounce her for giving false evidence? But Trivulzio never did this, neither at the beginning, nor later. In his article of 3 November, Todeschini quoted a news item in *Il Gazzettino di Venezia*. It reported the evidence of a pharmacist from Isola della Scala who attested to having heard from Policante that she had gone on Trivulzio's behalf to the midwife De Mori and offered her 300 lire to perform an abortion for a 'putela',* and that De Mori had written his name on the wall.

In another article on 10 November Todeschini attacked *Verona Fedele*, a clerical broadsheet which insisted on denying that the body was Isolina's. 'Our fellow editor persists in doubting the identity of the corpse and every time the name Isolina is printed, follows it with a question mark. We would like to ask the editor of this clerical broadsheet to get information from Lieutenant Trivulzio. This man, who replied to questions from Signor Felice Canuti, the victim's father, with "It's all right, you can be sure your daughter's in a safe place", ought to be able to say whether Isolina is alive or if she is somewhere which is unfortunately forever out of harm's way.'

A challenging article followed a few days later in which Todeschini reported that Trivulzio had joined the Royal Prosecutor in a lawsuit for damages against Cavalier Pietro Zamboni for 'disposing of a body'.

Todeschini's comment was: 'Not so fast, elegant officer! We would like to know if Policante's accusations against that respectable gentleman have somehow become more credible given that you have gone running to the Royal Prosecutor. You have never bothered him before this, nor have you ever asked him for any help, despite the fact that you are a man accused of devising ways of procuring an abortion for an unfortunate victim of you "officers and gentlemen".'

On 8 December, Todeschini really threw down the gauntlet with a decisive article aggressively entitled 'Take Lieutenant Trivulzio to court!'

*In Venetian dialect, a young girl.

'Please note, Signor lieutenant, we write: to court, not to prison. Our newspaper is not accusing you of murder, it is publicly accusing you of being a suspect in public opinion. And since we do not know whether the legally constituted Tribunal takes public opinion into account, it seems opportune to begin, or rather continue, proceedings against you in this newspaper.

'To court then: we shall conduct a debate in the hope that sooner or later you will start proceedings against us leading to a trial which, until now, you have failed to set in motion.

'We shall not ask for your personal details, these are of no interest to us, but shall begin the customary interrogation.

'On 23 January 1900, after suffering the terrible shock of an unexpected arrest, you wrote a letter from Scalzi Prison to your colonel. In this letter you talked about "fatal circumstances" which had implicated you in a crime.

'Is it therefore true that you were, let us say for the time being, a simple witness, implicated in a crime which caused the death of Isolina Canuti?

'Reply: We regret that we are unable also to write your series of replies for you. If you would like to reply, you always have *L'Arena* at your disposal.

'Question: You said in your letter that an inexplicable web of evidence was conspiring against you. Of all this evidence, so thick as to constitute a web, only one piece saw the light of day in your confession and that was your sexual relationship with Isolina Canuti. What are the others?

'Reply: . . .

'Question: Again in your letter to your colonel you say: if I were the guilty person, I would already have killed myself. By writing "the guilty person" you have made it evident that you knew who the guilty person might be, or else you would have written "if I were guilty". Your expression would indicate that you could unload the responsibility for the crime on to another person and that better still, you were advising that person to do his duty by killing himself. Is that so?

'Reply: . . .

'Question: It is noted in the proceedings of our preliminary investigation that a little while after Isolina Canuti's flight from the paternal home on 5 January, you said to Felice Canuti, putting an arm round his shoulder, "Rest assured Don Felice, Isolina is somewhere safe." So while her father was worrying and going around asking people, you knew where she was. So where was she? And if you know, why have you still not told us?

'Reply: . . .

'Question: What have you to say in your defence when faced with accusations made with maximum publicity, that you tried to find suitable ways of procuring an abortion for Isolina Canuti? It is noted in the proceedings that Isolina once said to you, "I took the powder but nothing happened." It appears that you also made great haste to go and see Maria Policante, because she was to look for a midwife who would take care of Isolina's abortion for you. Is all that true?

'Reply: . . .

'Question: What was your interest in procuring an abortion for Isolina Canuti? What impulse were you obeying when you told her that she either had to go to Milan to have the baby or stay here in Verona and have an abortion? Is it true that Isolina wanted to have the baby in the hope that with such a tie you would then be induced to marry her?

'Reply: . . .

'Question: Did you say that it seemed impossible to you that Isolina Canuti – a "scorpion" as you called her on one occasion – could have got pregnant?

'Reply: . . .

'Question: Is it true, as we have learned from a reliable source, that to overcome Policante's reluctance to look for a willing midwife you told her that you would spend money, supporting your offer with these words: "If you have money you can even find someone to kill a man?"

'Reply: . . .

'Question: It is known that you or your lawyers are taking the stand that Isolina Canuti was at a stage of her pregnancy which must have pre-dated your stay in the Canutis' house. We refute this hastily contrived, groundless defence and accuse you of making every effort to procure an abortion for Isolina whose pregnancy you feared would be an annoying responsibility, since you knew that she wanted to have a normal birth in the hope (or illusion), as we have said, of obliging you to marry her. What explanation can you give for this?

'Reply: . . .

'Question: Your intimacy with the Canuti family was a close one. You were able to be alone with Isolina even when her father was at home. The neighbours, on the other hand, were scandalized by such intimacy and told Signor Canuti the times when Isolina would go to your room and the time that she would spend with you. Her father did not take any more notice than usual and let you continue your love affair with Isolina in peace. And you used that freedom which Signor Felice allowed you as a reason for accusation – you accused her father in the judge's presence. But we would like to ask you if her father's behaviour authorized you to procure an abortion for Isolina? What do you have to say about that?

'Reply: . . .

'Question: To all of these questions you have never given any reply which would make them seem futile or bizarre, locked as you are in an obstinate silence – disdaining to proceed with a lawsuit which would be extremely useful to you (that is, if you really are innocent) since it would serve to give you that satisfaction of which they deprived you when they closed the preliminary investigation on you – you live merrily in San Briccio di Lavagno and let the world go hang. Is this what you want?

'Reply: . . .

'Question: Well then, keep silent, we shall pursue a trial. . . .'

IX

We return to the Trattoria Chiodo in Vicolo Chiodo. From the investigation carried out by *Verona del Popolo* several incongruous things emerged: for example, on the evening of the crime, one of the waiters was missing. The owner, Annibale Isotta, gave conflicting explanations about this to his customers: to one he said that the man was ill, to another that he was working in another restaurant, to a third that he was not working because he was on holiday.

Il Gazzettino di Venezia then got evidence from another inn-keeper called Gobbi, who said that Isotta had talked to him about what happened on the terrible night of 15 January.

But let us see how *Verona del Popolo* reconstructed the affair in an article by Todeschini.

'A few days after the discovery of some of the remains of the woman who had been cut up in pieces, it was rumoured that the crime had taken place at the Trattoria Chiodo. What people were saying also came out in the press. . . .

'Along with the bundle of human remains fished out at the Garibaldi Bridge there was a tablecloth which many people said was precisely the kind used at the Chiodo. But in fact it's possible to find tablecloths exactly like that in a variety of restaurants.

'Let us try, meanwhile, to examine the Chiodo, starting at the entrance and leaving aside those rooms that are of no interest to us.

'On the ground floor of the trattoria which is in a house at 9 Vicolo Chiodo, there are amongst the other rooms two rooms which are rather large. One, furnished in a rustic fashion, has walls that are decorated with about ten portraits. These are paintings of members of the Chiodo Society.

'Further on, there is another room, a little room where various officers of His Majesty's Army meet. These, we believe, are also members of the society.

'The owner of the trattoria, Annibale Isotta, lets out the second floor of the next house, no. 7. If you stay in the house, it's possible to have access to the rooms on this second floor, one of which serves as a little bathroom and has a tank and a tap from the water system. Behind the rooms on the ground floor which are used by the trattoria there is a courtyard. If you open a rough wooden door at the back of it and go down five little steps, you come into a room with an earthen floor which is used as a store-room and lumber room. In one corner of this is a chopping block used by the trattoria for cutting up pieces of meat which are taken from the kitchen to the customers.

'Finally, this room has a door which gives on to Vicolo Pomo d'Oro. Would this be the scene of the crime? Let's see. . . .

'On the evening of 14 January this year, a Sunday, the usual waiter was not at the Trattoria Chiodo. According to what the owner said first, the waiter had to serve at a dinner somewhere else. However, some time later the same owner said that his waiter was absent because he was ill.

'That evening, between nine and ten, first two officers, and then three more left the restaurant. At one particular moment, when the customers didn't need him to be there, the owner went out to the alley-way. He stood there with his legs wide apart for a little bit, and from time to time looked up at the lighted window on the second floor of the house, no. 7. He was surprised in this position by a person who suddenly passed by and who heard him cursing softly. Then he went back in.

'After the morning of 16 January when the miserable remains of Isolina were discovered, it was suggested that the Trattoria Chiodo was the likely scene of the crime. The above-mentioned person remembered all this and he thought he could explain Isotta's behaviour and the curses he was uttering by the fact that he had discovered what had happened.

'Obviously the innkeeper at the Chiodo did not share the burden of guilt of those responsible. And during those few days, which must have been terrible for him because of his fear of what the public might think, he confided in someone who had come to see him on business.

'He willingly agreed that this person who was curious to see all the rooms in the trattoria could do so, showing him first of all the room with the portraits and the names of some of the people represented, and then letting him see the room that the officers usually occupied.

'It was then that the visitor asked for some explanation for the current gossip about Isolina and the Chiodo and the officers. To which the innkeeper replied, "What more can I tell you, this is the room where it happened, whatever it was that happened.

They held her down and stuck a fork inside her and then whatever happened, happened. Afterwards they took her away to some other house."'

Meanwhile, an anonymous letter arrived at the offices of the newspaper *Verona del Popolo*. Todeschini did not take it seriously precisely because it was anonymous. But with the passage of time the things that were said in the letter appeared more and more likely because they were confirmed by other pieces of evidence.

The letter, later put forward at the Todeschini trial, explained how the crime happened: 'Some officers agreed on a dinner organized at the Trattoria Chiodo and they invited (or someone invited) Isolina Canuti and the other young woman who later died in hospital.

'When everyone was a bit high, one of them said, "Isolina, since you want an abortion, come and stretch yourself out on the table." Isolina obeyed because as she was drunk, she had no feeling of danger. Neither perhaps did the person who invited her to lie down on the table. It was then that the fork was introduced into her uterus and Isolina uttered a shrill scream from the terrible pain.

'They needed to stifle that scream which could possibly have alerted the attention of some passerby or certainly someone in one of the other rooms in the trattoria.

'So the hand of the person doing the "operation", or somebody else present, would have seized the tablecloth and gagged Isolina with it. Her body would still have been convulsed in agony. The poor creature would have tried to alleviate her suffering by screaming. But those screams would have compromised the men surrounding her, who were only conscious of their own danger (that of being discovered with a woman bleeding from her womb), and this made them take their time in releasing her from the tablecloth. They let her go only when she fell silent, and found themselves faced with a corpse. And so they had to think of a way in which they could erase all traces of the crime they had committed.

'The author of the anonymous letter states that he heard the story told by an ex-officer who said he knew everything that had happened, and that it was no mystery to other officers either.

'The words of the letter', continued Todeschini, 'are confirmed by the evidence of the landlord, Gobbi, who said exactly the same thing: "They held her down and stuck a fork inside her. . . ."'

On 24 December *Il Corriere della Sera* published a new piece of news on the Isolina case. 'A skull has been retrieved near Rondo on the Adige, in the Bosco neighbourhood.'

When it was brought into the Town Hall, the skull was analysed by a medical judiciary who stated that it was the greatly disfigured head of a young woman. It would have been twelve months in the water. One tooth remained and a bit of hair.

All the evidence suggested that it was Isolina's head. 'This confirms the news reported by a city newspaper that some boys playing by the river had dragged out a woman's head with two chestnut plaits attached to the scalp and that they had thrown it back into the water in horror.'

The *Corriere* forgot to add that the boys went to the police but were not believed. Or rather, they were told not to say anything about their gory discovery. This was what one of the boys said, and his story was reported in both *Il Gazzettino* and in *Verona del Popolo*.

At this point a crisis was reached. Todeschini's provocative articles on one hand, and the new discovery on the other, made Trivulzio's situation very difficult. If he did not proceed with a lawsuit then he would tacitly admit guilt, and if he did proceed he would have to undergo a public trial.

And yet many months were to pass, almost twelve, before Trivulzio brought an action against Todeschini.

PART TWO

In Isolina's Footsteps

I

Verona. Following Isolina. I arrive Thursday, 19 September, on the train from Rome. I go to the Cavour Hotel in Vicolo Chiodo. A narrow staircase, a minute room which gives on to a tiled roof, filmy white curtains, pigeons squabbling.

I am in the heart of Verona. I go down to explore the street. I ask for the Chiodo Restaurant. Not a trace of it remains. A shoemaker tells me 'I've worked here for thirty years but I've never seen a restaurant . . . I did hear that there was a trattoria here many years ago but they knocked it down. There's a new house there now.'

The street is grey, narrow and clean. There are a few doors which are barred, no shop except for the shoemaker's with its dark little room opening on to the pavement. At number 9 there is a door with glass panels and the name plate of an office.

At the end of the street, towards Via Cavour, is a freshly painted wall. In a corner is a bas-relief of a girl's small face. Stone on stone. The hair is tied back in a thick plait, the lips are full, the nose rather broad. The public wanted to see, in this little sculpture, the portrait of Isolina. It hangs half-way up the wall and has an air both wise and puzzled, with its empty eyes of grey stone and its cheeks eaten away by time.

In Vicolo Pomo d'Oro, on to which the other door of the Chiodo Restaurant led, there are no new houses. The entrances, all brass and glass, are new and like those of any office. No trace of a restaurant.

My friend Pippo Zappulla, who took part in my writing class at the Free University of Alcatraz in Santa Cristina, now takes me round the city to help me out and is developing a passion, tinged with the irony and candour which are so peculiarly his, for the case. He introduces me to his friends in Verona.

One of them, a lawyer named Guarienti, turns out to be very nice and makes himself immediately available, even though he has a great deal to do. He has a luxuriant moustache which overflows to join a curly beard, a wide receding forehead, ears which stick out and the thick glasses of the very short-sighted. He is well known in the city because he defends 'all the lost causes' as his friends call them; people who are miserably poor or persecuted, prostitutes, drug addicts. He has an overwhelming and infectious optimism. He is always smiling, knows everyone, has a ready wit, and is famous for his ostentatiously bright jackets. If you walk through Verona with him, you have to stop every moment: 'Hello lawyer, how's your wife?' 'How are you doing, Chips?' He calls everyone by their nickname.

And it is he who accompanies me to see Sebastiano Livoti, the president of the Tribunal, an amiable and cultured Sicilian who loves painting and literature and knows everything there is to know about music and history.

I ask him to help me find the files from the preliminary investigation on the Canuti case. And he, very kindly, calls the clerks and has them go through the warehouse. But not a trace of the preliminary investigation is to be found. 'It seems that everything must have been destroyed by fire,' he tells me. 'Try the State Archive.'

I go to the Archive. The director, a Signora Laura Castellazzo, receives me courteously. She listens to me. She goes and consults her card indexes. But she too finds nothing on the Canuti case. 'Try at the Central Library,' she finally suggests to me.

I go to the library in Via Cappello, skim through all the card indexes but find nothing there either. Meanwhile, the lawyer Guarienti tells me that he has succeeded in tracking down a clerk who worked at the Tribunal until a few years ago, before he became a pensioner. He would probably know more than anyone else: his whole life was spent dealing with the files on the trials in Verona.

The clerk says that he spent twenty years in the Tribunal's

archive and knew by heart the location of every file. 'And do you know anything about a file on the Canuti preliminary investigation?'

'I don't remember. But there's nothing there anymore because all the files were given away as waste paper to the Red Cross a few years ago.'

'Couldn't I go into the archive myself and have a look?' I insist stubbornly. The clerk starts to laugh.

'There's more dust than air in there. And it's full of rats.'

'I'm not afraid of rats.'

'I told you, there's nothing in there anymore, nothing.'

It seems incredible that important documents to do with the history of Verona have been thrown away like that, carelessly, on a foolish impulse and without a thought for their value. Or perhaps it was worse, perhaps it was done to prevent anyone from sticking their nose into the case?

'So, what's left on the Canuti case?' I ask. 'What documents are there for me to consult? And where did the documents of the Todeschini trial end up? I understand that nothing is left of the preliminary investigation, but what about the trial . . .'

'There's the sentence of the Todeschini trial. If you want to photocopy it, you can. There are the lawyers' speeches.'

'Isolina's lawyers?'

'No, Trivulzio's lawyers.'

'And what else can I consult?'

'Well, the only things left are the daily papers of the time with their journalistic accounts of the trial.'

Then I shall find nothing. I have already had the newspapers for the past two months and have studied them thoroughly. I have piles of photocopies on my desk. And photographs of the time, and letters, and books, but nothing specifically on Isolina.

I drive around with Pippo Zappulla and his wife Manuela in their little Fiat, searching for traces of Isolina. We do not want to give up.

The first thing we do is to go to the cemetery. We ask to see the register of the first few days of the century. The registers are all in order and it's easy to consult them. Almost ninety years of deaths on two very clean shelves. But in the enormous book in

which are recorded the deaths in the year 1900, there is no
Isolina Canuti.

We walk amongst the graves. We find a tombstone belonging
to the Spinelli family (Isolina's mother), but not even a cross
bearing the Canuti name.

'But where are the members of Isolina's family buried?' I ask
the watchman.

'They might be in the communal grave. Every ten years the
tombs are emptied and the bones thrown into the communal
grave.'

The cemetery is overflowing with tombstones and flowers. It
is hot. The sun has just appeared suddenly from behind white
clouds. There are massive tall columns around us. In front of us
is a kind of pantheon with the inscription PIIS LACRIMIS. We
walk round the gravel paths between ostentatious marble
graves covered with flowers. There is much rhetoric amongst
the engraved phrases of regret: 'sons overwhelmed by the loss
of their beloved mother', 'sisters longing for their Maria', 'husband of the most beloved wife', and so on.

Under glass are yellowed oval portraits of the torsos and
heads of women sitting stiffly upright, and men with wild
stares. Their dark eyes follow visitors with expressions sometimes ironic, sometimes worried, sometimes ecstatic. There are
wrinkled little faces, long beards faded by the damp, children
who smile unhappily.

In the middle of a semi-circle of columns is a broad grey
stone. This is the common grave. Above it sits a rusty little tin
can in which is a bunch of fresh flowers. Here they probably
threw Isolina's broken bones, reduced now to tiny fragments: a
bit of tibia, a chip of backbone, a phalanx, a small piece of
cranium.

There is something senseless about this rage directed at the
body of a pregnant young girl. Wiping out a life is not easy.
Something always remains which refuses to be destroyed, reduced to nothing. The Nazis knew very well that they did not
succeed in completely eliminating the bodies of the Jews. Every
day they would experiment with a new method: some thought
that burning them was the best method, but it was slow and the

ovens were expensive to run; others believed in corrosive acids; some proposed burying, others wet cement.

But the bones still remain, reduced to little pieces, as testimony to a body which was once alive despite every desire to annihilate it, and which continues to signal silently but decisively as if to say: It took nine months to give me form, it took years and years to make me an adult, years of work, of love, of sleep, of nourishment, and you cannot, you simply cannot eliminate me.

II

'Where do you think I might find something on Isolina Canuti's death?' I ask the watchman in the cemetery.

'Try the Police Mortuary.'

So Manuela, Pippo and I make our way along the road which skirts the cemetery as far as an iron gate on which 'Police Mortuary. Municipal Administration' is clearly written.

It is four o'clock. The office seems to be asleep beneath the lazy autumnal sun. They welcome us politely. They show us the files. It is moving to leaf through them, following the minute handwriting in the green ink of the period.

We look at all the pages, from January 1900 onwards. February, March, April . . . right to the end of the year. But Isolina's name does not appear. There is not even any indication that the bodies were recovered. Except in July, where an 'unknown body' is registered. And below this, barely visible: 'About 20. Female sex.' The date on which it was found: '5 July'.

It seems a desecration. Fingers, alive in 1983, gleaning dead and distant records. And here is an unusual entry: on 17 July the registrar notes the finding of a four-month-old foetus, male. Fished out of the Pedrigoni canal. What if it were Isolina's baby who was never found in the Adige?

Pieces of Isolina were found during different months, in different areas by various people. The head was found twelve months later. Why couldn't the foetus have been found six months later? But no one ever mentioned it.

There is no trace of Isolina, however. As far as the community registers go, she never existed. Perhaps she was born, but she never died.

And what became of her descendants? Isolina had three siblings. If they married, did they have children? What became of them?

I get the telephone directory. I look under Canuti. There are a few of them. I ring. The replies are unhelpful. They don't know who Isolina was, they are not related to her, they know nothing, and are not interested in knowing anything about her.

The last one I telephone is a Viscardo Canuti. The name reminds me of something. Now I remember: Isolina's younger brother was called Viscardo.

I telephone. He answers. A man with a sweet and pleasant voice. He says yes, they are related to Isolina, but he would prefer not to talk about her. I ask him for an appointment. At first he says no. Then he relents. 'OK, meet me tomorrow at the shop.'

I go with only Pippo this time. Manuela is busy with her work as a weaver. And then there is the baby, Francesco, who even though he is a good baby and an independent one, every so often demands his mother's presence.

The electrical goods shop has a glass door opening on to the street with the name Canuti displayed prominently. Every time the door is opened a bell jingles to announce the visitor.

Viscardo Canuti is inside, in an inner room behind an old mahogany table, between mountains of paper, lamps, sockets, cardboard boxes. I recognize him at once. He looks disturbingly like the portrait of Clelia, Isolina's sister, by the painter Dall'Oca Bianca.

There are the family features: a sharp face with a meek air, sloping shoulders, neck stretched forward, a long nose, pinched cheeks, gentle eyes which are extremely clear and full of curiosity.

By his side are his daughter and his grandson, Maria Luisa and Andrea. Both have the stamp of the Canuti-Spinelli family but with a robust, healthy look which Isolina and Clelia never possessed.

I ask Viscardo Canuti what memories they have of Isolina, if
he ever heard the family talk about her.

'She was your father's sister, wasn't she?'

'Yes. I know of her existence but the family never talked
about her. My mother used to say to me: if they ask you about
her, say you don't know her. Aunt Clelia I remember well. She
was a bit clumsy, she moved awkwardly. Have you ever seen
Rita Pavone's *Gianburrasca*? Well, in that film there was a
woman – I don't know what her name was, I think Tina Pica
played her – who was like Aunt Clelia. She walked as if her legs
were a bit bandy, she had a small head, a lot of hair, her face
always looked frightened. . . .'

'Did Aunt Clelia marry?'

'No, never. Only my father and Uncle Alfredo got married.
My mother's name was Maria Castagna and she had three
children. Bruna who was born in 1912, Eleanora in 1910 and me
in 1914.' He answers me with a kind of fussy precision, a note of
pride in his voice. 'I then married Antonia Brunelli and we have
had four children: Gianfranco born in '39, Annabella in '44,
Maria Luisa in '54 and Marinella in '61. Gianfranco is the only
one who has got married up till now and he has a son, Andrea.
Do you want to look at a photograph?'

'What do you remember about your father, Viscardo?'

'He was a nice man, a good man. My uncle Alfredo was a
captain in the artillery. We were on good terms with Uncle
Alfredo, we used to see one another all the time.'

'And did he sometimes talk about Isolina?'

'No, never. It was forbidden in the family to talk about her.
No one was even to know that we were relatives of that poor
little thing.'

'And what do you know about Isolina, even if it's only what
you've heard other people say?'

'She was a lively girl. And she got pregnant. They wanted to
make her have an abortion. The thing went badly. To cover up
the crime they had her cut up in pieces.'

'And what do you remember about your grandmother,
Giuseppina Spinelli?'

'She was a silent woman, small, cautious and determined.

But she died too soon . . . I don't remember much.'

The curious thing about this family is that over three genera-
tions not one woman married. Isolina died tragically. Clelia
lived with her nieces and nephews. Viscardo's two daughters,
Bruna and Eleonora are not married.

Signor Canuti disappears for a moment and returns after a bit
with a photograph of Giuseppina Spinelli. He puts it in front of
me with an emphatic gesture. 'Here's my grandmother, she
looks like Isolina.'

A severe face, bordered by a rather funereal oval frame. The
fixed and unmoving expression of an era when photographs
were taken rarely and then only on special occasions. A
herring-bone woollen dress fastened at the neck with a bow
made out of fur. A rectangular brooch which stands out on the
black dress. The face turned towards the camera. A minute,
oval face with regular features, an aquiline nose, fine lips,
deep-set eyes which are rather close together. Large ears. Hair
parted in the middle, combed down on to the forehead and
then drawn back behind the temples into a single massive plait.

'The Canuti family were of noble origin. They were rich once,
but lost all they owned when Napoleon expropriated everything.'
Viscardo Canuti tells me this as he opens a large bound book.

'The first Canuti, in fact Canuto, came from Bologna and
belonged to a royal family. Guglielmo Canuti held the con-
sulship in Bologna in 1283. Another Canuti, Lorenzo, was professor of anatomy at the University of Bologna. Then a branch
of the family settled in Verona. It's all written down here in this
book. It's possible that it's not true . . . but I think it is. . . .'

He looks at me with his small luminous eyes, like those of a
child. He shows me the emblem of the Canuti family on the
book which is bound in red morocco leather: a dog looking at a
tree. Green on blue. Three stars in one corner.

It is time to say goodbye. He tells me he has to go. He shakes
my hand politely. He is not suspicious. He does not even ask
me what I shall write. He rewards me with a beautiful, trusting
smile, for which I am grateful.

III

My pilgrimage continues. From one station to the next, in the footsteps of Isolina and Trivulzio. Where did they go, what did they do, whom did they see? It is difficult to track down the images of a dead city behind the façade of a modern city, which has been deformed, transformed and even blown up.

The Pallone Barracks where Trivulzio was stationed no longer exists. In its place is a modern street of anonymous little buildings. The bridges were blown up by the Germans in the last war. The house in Via Cavour where the Canutis lived has been pulled down. Where it stood is the dark glass door of a very modern bank. The Chiodo Restaurant: vanished.

It seems that the city has put all its energies into destroying every trace of its wretched daughter.

With Manuela and Pippo I go in search of the Pericolanti School where Isolina was put immediately after her mother died. In fact, its real name is San Silvestro Institute, but it came to be called Pericolanti* because it took in orphans who were in danger, whether of dying from starvation or 'losing their virtue', I don't know. Perhaps both.

We stop in front of a yellow two-storey stonebuilt house. It's rather pretentious with its entrance surmounted by a crescent-shaped architrave and flanked by two fluted stone columns. The windows are framed with white stone. Iron grilles give them a prison-like air.

The Mother Superior receives us, a small lean young woman who seems extremely suspicious. She asks us what we are looking for. But she pretends not to remember anything about Isolina Canuti. She tells me that I have probably made a mistake in thinking that she was here. However, the registers of the final years of the nineteenth century can't be found, they have probably been destroyed. And so it is futile for me to insist.

But I do insist. She tells me that she will have a look, and let me know. I know from her face that she will not do anything, that she is in a hurry to send us away, that she is mistrustful.

---

*Pericolanti: lit., those who are unsafe

I ask her about the convent's history. Sitting on the edge of her chair, she answers courteously but coldly, in a voice which sounds metallic: 'In 1200, there was an ancient Benedictine convent here. The Benedictine sisters ran it from 1200 until 1600. Then the Penitents replaced them. They were lay people who were ready to lead a new life and isolated themselves in cells. After this, it became a reformatory for young girls who came from all over Italy, even from Rome. Then the Order of the Sisters of Maria Bambina, to which I belong, replaced it. Our Order has been here for 130 years. Our president is a Bishop and he presides at Brescia.'

I ask if I might visit the school. She tells me that it is not possible. 'In a short while it will be a mealtime, so you'll understand. . . .'

I take two steps towards the courtyard. Alarmed, she comes up behind me, but she can't stop me from looking.

I look out on to a very beautiful sunny courtyard enclosed on all sides by wide windows. On one side is a bright corridor. And then suddenly another courtyard, this time open to the sky, with a gigantic magnolia in the middle.

I can't stop myself from imagining Isolina as a child, dressed in her grey school clothes, playing ball with her friends. I see her running wildly about the square courtyard. I see her suddenly tired, her cheeks pale with anaemia, as she leans panting, ball in hand, against the magnolia. The hump of her spine rests awkwardly against the rough trunk. But she does not care. She wants to play so much that even this shabby courtyard seems a park to her and this tree a sequoia, boldly uniting Verona's earth and sky.

I hear footsteps. Two little girls pass by timidly holding hands. They have books under their arms. Socks fallen down around their calves, shining eyes. The Sister makes a sign to me as if to say: That's enough, this visit is really at an end, now go away.

We follow her reluctantly towards the exit. I would have liked to see the dormitory, the refectory. I would have liked to hear the suppressed laughter, the buzzing, the murmurings of that small and restricted female world so similar to the Florentine boarding school where I spent three years of my adolescence, so similar to all boarding schools, monasteries, convents, in which women have grown up over the centuries.

From the school I go to the Officers' Club. This is right behind the old castle. An old wooden drawbridge full of holes. Chains covered with creepers. And a ditch opening up at one's feet, bristling with thistles and weeds.

Inside it is dark. A corridor to a room with a shining marble floor. Frosted glass doors, heavy velvet curtains, beaded lamp-shades hanging from the centre of the ceiling.

I ask a waiter if I might visit the Officers' Club room. He says that he has to ask the captain. Where is the captain? He is having a drink with friends. Is it possible to get him? Yes, perhaps, he was here a moment ago. And he goes out silently.

The captain comes in. A good-looking man with a crew cut, a tanned face. I ask him if I can visit the Club. He looks askance at me. Why? he asks without curiosity. I tell him that I am doing research on ancient buildings in Verona. I can't explain the whole story about Isolina.

Courteously, but with visible annoyance, he tells me, 'Of course, the waiter will accompany you.' And goes back to his friends.

We go down a long corridor off which are windowless rooms of varying sizes. At the bottom on the left is a jumble of scattered tables. The French windows give on to a long narrow terrace covered with plants and flowers. The terrace leans languidly towards the Adige. Mud-coloured water runs tumultuously below. 'In summer the officers eat outside here. Nice view, eh?'

We turn back. The waiter opens the door of a ballroom with wood-panelled walls. There are large seventeenth-century oil paintings on the walls, a chandelier with a thousand branches hangs miraculously overhead, a piano, chairs, tables piled up.

As I am walking towards the exit, I stop for a moment to look through a half-closed door at the captain and his friends. They are sitting around a metal table in a little courtyard thick with flowers. A kind of hanging garden on the terraces of the castle. They are smiling at one another, talking animatedly, raising their glasses to their lips. The tone, the rhythm, the emotional intensity of the meeting brings to mind those long ago meetings when Lieutenant Trivulzio came here to play cards with his friends, and the civilian world seemed so far away to them, so slavish and corrupt from inside these ancient walls, like a world of brokers and money-lenders.

You can breathe this feeling of belonging to a special caste in the very air. You can feel it in the captain's confident gestures, in his bored tanned face, in the arrogant smiles of the other officers, in the crystal glasses which shine on the immaculate tablecloth, in the intimidated behaviour of the waiter who tries to adapt himself to a ceremony which is fundamentally alien to him and yet fascinating.

The visit is at an end. We go back to the city which is suffocating from its traffic, from the exhaust fumes and the smell of wine and dirt which emanates from the ruins of old entrance halls.

Another day has passed. I climb the stairs which lead to the little room in Vicolo Chiodo. It seems to me that I fail to understand the meaning of this search which nevertheless continues to intrigue and fascinate me.

I fall asleep in a few minutes and dream anguished dreams of rivers in full flood and of women's bodies floating in the current.

IV

The next day, we start at the Adige. Manuela, large eyes shining, grey hair shaped like a helmet, is the driver of the Fiat. I sit alongside her with my notebooks, my books, my camera. We make our way towards Ponte Aleardi. There we park and continue on foot.

I look out over the water which runs rapidly over a bed of grey sand. Rusty iron gates, an art nouveau glass roof with bits broken off. An atmosphere both seductive and funereal. Acacia trees of a clear, almost liquid green through which you can see bits of the wall of the old city.

The current carries away everything in its path, creates whirlpools, drags chunks of wood, rubbish. Seagulls, which here are called *cocai*, fly low, making strident, raucous cries.

It is so easy to imagine a bundle carried along by the current, eddies of greenish water turning it around, branches holding it back. And the washerwomen who run up to open the bundle, convinced that it is smuggled meat. And then, the terrible shock on the two motherly faces as they are confronted with that display of pieces of female flesh.

We go on and rejoin the nineteenth-century Garibaldi Bridge. Solid white granite and red brick walls. A riverbed of clean white stones. Green mildew eating away at the granite, making it less compact and rigid, as if bearing witness to time's passing.

At one o'clock we have an appointment with the lawyer, Guarienti, who takes us up the Torricelle mountain to eat spaghetti. The view over Verona opens up like a softly coloured fan in the delicate yet vibrant tints of a Japanese painting. Something unreal. Like whole cities, upside-down, shining palely green, reflected in the clouds on the horizon.

A magnificent immobility. One that wipes out every disgrace, every crime, in a dizzying glassy eternity.

In the afternoon, we take the Fiat to Ronco on the Adige, the place where Isolina's head was found. We struggle behind in her faint tracks, picking up the little stones that she sowed on her road towards the world of the dead.

When we arrive it is almost dark and we make our way through extremely beautiful little villages like miniature cities – artificial lakes, castles, towers, drawbridges and trees centuries old.

We leave the car and go on along the river bank, amongst junipers and reeds alongside newly planted ploughed fields. Here the water is deep and makes menacing whirlpools. Willows and hawthorns grow untidily along the banks.

Isolina's disfigured head was fished out here. A plait of chestnut hair still attached to the skin, eye sockets close together, a small and well-formed jaw. It had spent twelve months immersed in the water of the river.

We go back because it is supper time. We have an appointment with a friend, called Bertani, who is a publisher. We wait
for him in Piazza Erbe in front of a flower shop. He arrives with
a confident manner, his red hair tousled by the wind, his
moustache worthy of a grenadier.

We eat together in an old trattoria, Il Cristo, where you can
still eat *la piarà*, creamed bread and veal marrow-bone with
black pepper.

Bertani eats heartily and looks his table companions straight
in the eye. He is as always, argumentative and candid. He says
that instead of occupying myself with a dead person in whom
no one is interested, I ought to write instead about someone
alive, Paola Elia, whose book entitled *Autogolpe* he has published. I promise him that I shall read the book.

'You must read it, she writes divinely, and then she was the
victim of a conspiracy – she is not in fact a spy as they say. Her
husband makes accusations against her but she is above all
that. . . . She is an exceptional woman, I would like you to meet
her.'

He promises to make me a present of some photographs of
Verona in 1900 which form part of his huge collection. I think he
is saying this just for the sake of it, because he looks distracted.
But then he does it. I see him arrive panting at the station on the
last day, a few minutes before the train leaves for Rome, with
an enormous package under his arm, a comical and sweet smile
on his lips.

V

A few steps from the Vicolo del Chiodo and Via Cavour is Villa
Canossa, an austere and very elegant building. A small inner
courtyard connects the street with the river.

I go in through an iron gate, the one that provoked such
arguments at the time of the Todeschini trial. Someone said
they had seen it open at night, while the night watchman

maintained that he always shut it at eight o'clock in the evening. The fact is that someone (witnesses Coronato and Cameri) saw two men carrying bags enter the courtyard of the Villa Canossa.

From the courtyard you go down two little steps to a long, ivy-covered balcony. I rest on the white granite parapet. I lean out over the river. The wall falls straight down to the water, which on this side of the villa is deep and runs rapidly.

From this parapet, according to a story told by Sitara himself (Trivulzio's orderly) to a friend who then told other people (evidence from Corbellari, Della Chiara, Graziani, Lizzari), he threw a bag into the Adige on the orders of his lieutenant.

It was a quiet night, the 14th of January, 1900. After Sitara looked at his hands, which were sticky and saw, in the lamplight, that they were covered with blood, he would have hurried to hurl the compromising bag off the balcony.

If you hold your breath, you can still hear the plop the bag made as it fell into the water in the night silence. It took a moment. Then the bundle was swallowed up by whirlpools and dragged away by the current.

I stop for a moment in the centre of the courtyard and look at the curious friezes that decorate the walls: deer running, bishops' mitres, spectacles, dogs lying down.

This beautiful building is closed behind the friezes, behind the high impenetrable grilles, behind the large diamond-paned leaded windows, with the indifferent solemnity of someone wanting to shut out every human event as too painful, too insistent.

Who knows if on that evening someone at one of the windows saw two shapes come up to the parapet? But probably even if they had seen something, they would not have talked. Like so many others who also knew, but kept their mouths shut. In the face of all the accusations, the military, the nobility, and the ruling class in the city all hid behind a proud and haughty silence.

From here we make our way to the judicial prison. The old Scalzi building no longer exists; it has been destroyed. To commemorate it a piece of remaining wall has been set in bricks on a beautiful communal lawn.

Where the old prisons once were there are now shops, a garage, a sports centre, little gardens. To the left rises the yellow body of the church of Santa Teresa di Avila. A restored seventeenth-century façade. At the top a saint holds a pen in her hands. A little angel holds up a book for her. Another hands her a sword.

Trivulzio was imprisoned here for a few days on the orders of the chief constable of Verona who was the first to interrogate him and to be convinced of his guilt. Who knows how many times Trivulzio might have raised his eyes to the saint with her pen and book clutching the top of the church!

Now there are only a few things left in the city for me to see and they particularly concern Trivulzio, the places where he was on picket-duty on the night of the crime: Fort Procolo, the Spagna Gunpowder Magazine.

No one knows where Fort Procolo is. I find it on a map of 1849 in the north-west of the city, to the left of the Adige, in front of those famous serpentine meanderings which carry the river towards the sea.

We drive over to the area in the Fiat, the car full of books and papers. We make enquiries at a barracks. They send us somewhere else and from there to yet another place.

Finally we are behind a courtyard of a barracks, behind a football field: Fort Procolo is now half-ruined. It springs up out of the ground like a stone mushroom.

We are not allowed to go any further because it is a military zone. 'The army uses it as a lorry depot. But rules are rules. The fort is fenced off and it is forbidden to go near it.'

A pleasant officer with blond curls takes us to the boundaries of barbed wire in the middle of brambles and oak saplings.

The abandoned and ruined fort has something solemn and pathetic about it. Its elegant lines are interrupted, its proportions spoilt, the bold play of height and space has given way to avalanches of soil and brambles.

I spend the evening looking through a book given to me by the director of a savings bank, a Dr Padovani, on historic military buildings in Verona. And so I discover the magnificence and beauty, now destroyed, of this former military city.

Fort Nugent, Fort Piovezzano, Fort Arona, Fort Prinz Rudolf, Fort Gisela, Fort Radetzky, Fort San Zeno, all are architectural masterpieces. Star-shaped, diamond-shaped, in the form of crosses, parallelograms, these fortresses have the absolute elegance and marvellous regularity of a militarism that reflects the vision of an absolutist and anthropocentric world.

Autocratic societies have always known how to create the greatest delights for the eye: magnificent monuments that take one's breath away, symmetries inspired by the perfection of the stars, massive yet delicate bodies, which play daringly with light and air even when their purpose is defence and military aggression.

A mystery to be resolved: the most perfect structures are the offspring of tyrants and mass murderers. Pyramids, temples, obelisks, churches, forts, towers, castles, palaces, monuments – beauty married to arrogance and despotism. It would be curious to find out the architectural offspring of playfulness and humility. But the future is silent.

In 1900, Verona was a garrison city in which the military were more numerous than civilians. A city bristling with towers, turrets, forts, gunpowder magazines, barracks. The inhabitants of these military buildings considered themselves the true sons of the city, the ones who gave it its class and style.

On the other hand, all Italy was divided into rich and poor, noble and plebeian, militarist and pacifist, socialist and conservative. It had just ended a ferocious and suicidal war in Ethiopia, a war that ended badly with an atrocious defeat at Adua where 8,000 lives were lost. King Umberto was an indecisive man, Queen Margherita a conservative bigot. In 1898 Di Rudini had permitted the most severe repression of popular uprisings (Bava Beccaris in Milan where cannons fired upon the crowd and 80 unarmed people were killed). The socialists Costa, Bissolati, Anna Kuliscioff and Turati were arrested. The universities were shut down together with the labour unions.

But finally the Di Rudini government had to be dismissed. The king, with his usual fearfulness and hesitation, made things worse by electing to government General Pelloux, whom he thought could rule the country with special powers and royal decrees.

In 1900 the king was assassinated. In this way the anarchist Bresci considered the victims of Bava Beccaris to be avenged. The bourgeoisie's minstrel, the restless D'Annunzio, moved from right to left with elegant ease.

In this atmosphere of fear and repression Verona amused itself. There were six good theatres in the city: the Filarmonico, the Ristori, the Manzoni, the Drammatico, the Arena and the Gambrinus, which continually put on opera, operettas, plays and various cultural spectacles.

The first film projection was enormously successful with the public. At the Ristori they showed big historical or mythological films accompanied by puppet shows, singing or dancing.

And an evening at the Grande Guardia included 'Experiments with Edison's phonograph', 'Pathé cinematographic projections', a 'Battle of the Gauls', a 'Sarah Bernhard Exhibition', a 'programme of Scottish dancing' and the 'Café Chanson from Paris'. All in one evening for the price of half a lira.

There were about ten private clubs. Amongst the most well known: the Verona, the Bel Tempo, the Veronetta, the Gran Via, the Folletto.

Many beer-houses existed, about ten or so. The most famous: the Margherita, the Europa, the Italia.

For those who preferred Cafés Chansons there was ample choice, a good eight just inside the city walls. And they welcomed singers from all over the world.

Every evening dances would be organized in the most famous villas: the Pullé, Musella, Chievo, the Theatre Club, the Chalet Can de la Scala, among others.

This is to say nothing of the masked balls, the most magnificent of which was held at the Sammicheli Salon and had ice-skating and an all-night party where everyone had to be dressed in white.

In the day time those who wanted to amuse themselves could go for a walk in the woods, venture as far as the famous Fontana di Ferro and drink water that was said to be miraculous for the liver. You could go to a horse race at the Madonna dell'Uva Secca or the races at the Velodromo, or simply take the air along the Adige.

When people took their evening stroll, you could see the most modern carriages going back and forth, from a victoria to a landau, a horse-and-four to a giardiniere, a brougham to a phaeton.

The officers led a frantically gay life, dragging along with them for entertainment girls they considered of little import-ance who, if they became pregnant, would not demand mar-riage. The young women from good families were kept well locked-up in their palaces, and when they did emerge for some ball at the Villa Canossa or the Officers' Club, would always be accompanied by aunts, mothers, grandmothers and cousins who never let them out of sight.

For girls who had more freedom because they were poorer, the temptations were such that they were almost irresistible. How could you say no to the poised, extravagant courting of so many officers who hid their brutality beneath impeccable man-ners and glittering uniforms?

To race down dusty roads on a bicycle, sowing terror amongst the hens and geese; to attend a horse race wearing a new jacket and see so many beautiful young ladies with their hair covered in flowers and fruit; to glide over the ice whirling around in the middle of a colourful crowd of young officers; to have dinner by candlelight in a well-known restaurant like the Chiodo or the Torcolo; to kiss in a dark hallway as carriages rolled by outside . . . what could be more seductive for a rest-less girl greedy for life?

Everywhere you went you were met by dozens of dashing officers with blond moustaches, sparkling eyes, bodies sheathed in fantastic uniforms the colour of green meadows, gold, forget-me-nots, blood. How could you resist the urge to throw yourself headlong into the parties, to play, to fall in love, to let yourself go?

VI

With an image of Isolina's tiny crooked body tightly corseted in an embroidered bodice spinning around in a whirling waltz, I go off to look for the Spagna Gunpowder Magazine where Trivulzio said he had spent the hours when the crime was committed.

It seems the Spagna Gunpowder Magazine is nowhere to be found. Some people say: 'It's over there, where the Pallone Barracks used to be'; others say 'No, it's opposite the bridge'. Someone sends us out into the countryside. Someone else sends us back to an abandoned slaughterhouse.

Finally, after going round and round we suddenly find it in front of us, on one side of the ramparts, enclosed by a shabby garden on one side and a line of modern houses on the other. The garden next to the ramparts is littered with used syringes, condoms and dog shit.

I climb up on to a piece of the old wall in order to take a photograph of the gunpowder magazine which lies behind a barred entrance. Behind me are cheap new houses with identical balconies and washing hung out to dry.

Beyond a high wall is the Spagna Gunpowder Magazine for which we have searched so hard. Enclosed in its little overgrown garden, it makes you think of the Sleeping Beauty. A long brick building punctuated by little windows with cornices of white stone. No glass. Only railings which make it vaguely resemble a prison.

The walls are swallowed up by swathes of creepers which climb up to the roof in a luxuriance of dark and dusty leaves. Tufts of stinging nettles and wild grasses spring out of the holes in the roof.

To the right is a little tower on two floors which can be reached by an external staircase. The only window is choked, like a mouth vomiting rotten leaves.

A door opens. Two feet shod in suede come forward with a soft noise like leaves being crushed. Two beautiful legs encased in ochre-coloured stockings advance into the darkness of a room hung with spiders' webs. The gloved hand holds the hilt of a silver sword which cuts down branches blocking the way.

A young man advances confidently. In the half-darkness, a glimpse of a black velvet hat tight on his temples, a plume of soft white feathers bending to his shoulder and dancing on his slender neck with every step. A velvet jacket, a shirt open at the neck. A languid face. Two curious liquid eyes.

The prince crosses the deserted corridors, the frozen rooms, trampling on broken glass, ants' nests. He climbs the stairs leading to the upper floors. He goes into one room and then another. And there, at the back of a dark still room, in a bluish light lies Sleeping Beauty, her body covered by her blonde hair, in which spiders are playing.

Moved, the prince stops and looks at Sleeping Beauty in her moth-eaten dress, with her transparent cheeks, her bloodless lips. He bends and with a light and delicate movement rests his blood-red lips on her dead ones.

In such a way Lieutenant Trivulzio kissed his lover and brought her back to life for us. But the moment he woke her he was terrified by what he had done. And now with real fear he watches her get up. Where will Sleeping Beauty go? To the tribunal, to the church, to the newspapers? What will she say about him? Beauty is so quiet and reassuring when it is dead!

Dead tired, I go back to the inn in Via del Chiodo that evening. It feels as though I have moved boulders during the day. Digging up the past is difficult and gives you a slight sense of nausea. It is like entering the world of the dead, who suddenly become intransigent, gossipy and greedy. They want you to remember them according to the ideas they had about themselves. They drag you here, there and everywhere without a pause to rest from their nagging requests.

Trivulzio, for example, is a dead person who is extremely demanding. He has sent me a packet of photographs through a friend of his, a Lucia di Stefano whom I have managed to contact through a woman from Udine.

In these photographs he looks me straight in the eye with the arrogance and confidence of an innocent unjustly condemned. In one photograph he wears the hard hat of a colonel, with fretwork and a stylized eagle sticking out of a dark ribbon. On his shoulders, insignia, a line of decorations on his chest. His face clean-shaven, the jaw wide, square, the eyes large and beautiful, the lips elusive, a sardonic smile which is barely perceptible.

In other photographs he is more relaxed. He takes up poses which are less official-looking, his face is calm and smiling, as in a small one taken quickly on the street in some little town in the mountains, near Udine. In the background, snow-covered peaks are visible. In the foreground Trivulzio is all dressed in dark woollen clothes, knickerbockers, a little felt hat. He holds a walking stick in his hand. On his feet, big mountain boots.

Near him, and it is the only instance of this, two people can be seen; a woman (his sister-in-law Ida) inelegant in a summer dress, also with a stick in her hand, her face looking backwards smiling slightly; at her side a man in uniform. He too is smiling at the photographer, who must be a friend, because it is a smile of amused complicity.

This is the only photograph in which Trivulzio appears in civilian clothes. The others, and there are so many, all show him in uniform. Almost always alone, sometimes with other soldiers. His beard long, at first black and then white, hair short and then very short, moustache thick, turned up, neglected, puffing out above his lips, cut cleanly or elongated towards his ears. With a sword, a riding crop, in long black boots, in brown riding boots.

In one photograph his hair appears to have been really cropped. He is seated in an armchair. His hands are two fists held in his lap. He is wearing a military coat with two little stars on the cuffs and on the collar. His expression is tired and tense, his eyes look away into the distance, his neck is swollen, cheeks soft and overlapping the stiff collar.

In another he is all dressed up as a hussar, with a dark jacket decorated with braid. In his hands – one is gloved and the other bare – he holds the hilt of a sword. On his head a peaked cap with a golden eagle. Clean-shaven, with only a well-groomed moustache which extends towards his cheeks. He looks straight ahead with a severe but satisfied expression.

At the bottom is a dedication: For Sub-Lieutenant Gino Yanod, Affectionately, Carlo Trivulzio. The signature is clear, with well-formed letters leaning slightly to the right. One sign of arrogance: the 'T' of Trivulzio, which overshoots the other letters in a determined thrust.

In another he looks like a rabbi. He wears a little black cap low down on his forehead, a fan-shaped white beard covers half his face and even his neck and part of his chest.

These are photographs of Trivulzio as an old man, aged 60 and over. The date of his death was 1949, when he was 73. Accompanied always by his untidy moustache and his uniform, we find him in Africa, then in Turin, then in Udine.

As he grows older, his broad face with its heavy features takes on a fragile, frightened aspect. But he does not lose that look of someone who feels himself protected by a paternal and loving God.

VII

From the country of the dead, Trivulzio has also sent me a friend's voice. A husky, broken voice. It belongs to Bruno Ballico, aged 83, a pensioner living in Udine who was formerly an engineer.

Without seeing his face, I listen to it by pressing the button on a tape recorder. He talks affectionately about his vanished friend, and is followed by the sweet clear voice of Lucia di Stefano who believed and believes in Trivulzio's innocence, without knowing anything, with the simple trust of friendship.

'"It is my wish", says Ballico, "that the truth will emerge from this research. Because Carlo Trivulzio suffered a great deal unjustly. He was an honest, courageous and discreet man. The last memory I have of him concerns the 8th of September.* He was preoccupied, he was asking himself if the army would ever again become as it was before and if his country would return to the way he knew it. I hope that the publishing house which is

*Date on which Fascism ended.

publishing your book is not leftist, because Trivulzio had terrible problems due to the socialists.

'"They brought an action because he came from a noble
family and because he was an excellent officer. It was an action
against the military and a particular way of seeing things.

'"He went away to Africa, to make a new life after the trial, to
the Colonies, and he was so respected that he was promoted to
general. He was a man who had certain values. He suffered a
great deal after the 8th of September. The fact that he left the
8th Alpini regiment all his property shows how attached he was
to the army. Everything that he owned he left to the Alpini."

'"But didn't he have a family and children? Wasn't he
married?"'

'"No, he never married. It seems that he never had a woman,
a lover. He lived in extreme seclusion, in the house of his
brother and sister-in-law. He was very affectionate towards
them. It was they who took care of his practical needs. When he
became ill his sister-in-law looked after him. They say that he
had cancer, but I don't know. He came from an old family from
Udine. The mother was a Verzegnassi. The brother Ludovico,
to whom he was so attached, had married a Haan of Austrian
origin. The ones who constructed the Ponteban railway."'

The same black tape recorder makes me the gift of another
voice. This is Dr Rizzi, aged 82, who was a cousin of Ida Haan,
and attended the Trivulzio household for a long time.

'"It wasn't a happy family," says the doctor. "Of the three
Trivulzio brothers, Carlo never married, Ludovico married but
had no children, Luigi had one girl, but she was so thin and
ugly that she never had a husband.

'"This girl, the family's sole heir, had asked to go and live
with her uncle Ludovico in Udine because she had suffered
poverty in Turin. But the uncle refused to take her in. Her aunt
Ida, on the other hand, would have taken her in willingly. This
child died of encephalitis, perhaps twenty years ago, without
marrying and therefore without heirs. It is unknown if encephalitis is hereditary or if it happens by chance. The fact is
that the uncle, Ludovico, had also had encephalitis. The Coun-
tess Bianca del Conte Rampolla Roncioni who used to live in Via

Sarvognana near Via Calzolati remembers the games that she played with the little Trivulzio girl when Luigi's daughter still lived in Udine. She remembers her wearing glasses; that she was very short-sighted, an ugly little thing who was not very healthy but extremely lively and high-spirited."

'"But why did Uncle Ludovico disinherit the little girl?"

'"He disinherited her because he hadn't approved of his brother Luigi's marriage. Not because of the difference in social position, but because his wife's morals left much to be desired."

'"You told me that the Trivulzio family came from Brescia."

'"Yes, it was a noble family from Brescia which was uprooted to Udine. The Udinese memoirs by the Amasei, which date from 1508 to 1541, mention the Trivulzio family. The mother was a Verzegnassi. There were three sisters. Two didn't marry. They stayed home with Laura, Carlo Trivulzio's mother. One day they say that they made the only brother drink something and had him sign a statement in which he undertook to give up the house. After this the brother instituted proceedings against the sisters, which lasted seventeen years."

'"And did you ever hear them talk about the proceedings in which Carlo Trivulzio was involved? What did the family say about that?"

'"I don't remember anything about the proceedings, I was too small. But I do know that it completely changed his character. Everyone said so. Before he was sociable, cheerful; afterwards he became closed, solitary, reluctant to talk to people even though he always behaved like a gentleman."

'"He was very fond of his brother's wife, Ida Haan. They were very close. It was she who took care of him when he fell ill. And when he died he left her the use of all his property. On her death it should have gone to the Alpini. He died in '49, she in '72. But everything is still up in the air. The army has been unsuccessful in getting hold of the inheritance."

'"When did you know him?"

'"I knew him in 1915 when he came back to Rome with eye injuries. He had been in the war, the 1915–18 war, as an Ardito,*

*Ardito: Military Fascist

he wore a black jersey with a skull on it; he was very brave. After the war he was unhappy, both because of his eye injuries and because he had lost all his diaries."

'"Perhaps we could have learned something about what he thought about the lawsuit from those diaries. Then the Trivulzio family completely died out. . . ."

'"Completely. The lawsuit also ruined his brother Ludovico who was secretary to the local council. He was a very intelligent man, with a degree in law. But he caught encephalitis and was finally very ill."

'"How did he catch it?"

'"We don't know, but he had been bitten by a tsetse fly in Gorizia."

'"What symptoms did he have?"

'"He was always sleeping. He had difficulty with words. He wrote a lot. But then he got drowsy and fell asleep. His brother Carlo was always with him. When I knew Carlo he had just come back with a long beard from Eritrea. He had let it grow to impress the Africans. Then when he came back to Italy he cut it off. He was a courageous soldier. He won a heap of medals on the battlefield. He was a fine-looking man, tall and imposing. But because he had been wounded in his eyes, he had a rather lifeless gaze. He was very energetic, very active, very nice, but reserved in everything. He often came to our house – he liked to joke, laugh, but always with a certain distance."

'"But did he die of pneumonia or cancer?"

'"He died heroically. He had a tumour of the stomach but he didn't want doctors and didn't take care of himself."

'"Do you think that he wanted to die?"

'"No, he died as he lived, courageously. His will said that he wanted to be cremated but since if you cremate someone you can't have a funeral, we asked the bishop's permission and he said, of course, had he talked to me when he was alive, he wouldn't have asked for a cremation. So we gave him a normal funeral and buried him in the Verzegnassi tomb."

'"But I noticed that there's no tomb with his name on it at the cemetery."

'"I don't know why his name's not there. I know that he's in the tomb belonging to his mother's family."

'"And did he never have a woman, a lover?"

'"He always lived alone. He never had sweethearts, women, nothing. When he was young he was very . . . he liked to enjoy himself. He was good-looking, he was much sought after by women. Then nothing. He shut himself up inside and lived the life of a Carthusian monk."

'"But who took care of him? He must have had someone to help him, someone who did the cooking and washing?"

'"My cousin, that is, his sister-in-law, took care of him. He was always with them. They bought the Fiumicello house together, which he then left to the Alpini. He left it so that it could be made into a rest-home for them. But nothing has yet been done about it. Peasants live there now."

'"And he never talked to you about the proceedings?"

'"Never. I know that he always suffered. But he never talked about it. I knew from my cousin. He confided in her. They were very attached to each other. He often slept at her house. He stayed to eat, morning and night, with his brother and his sister-in-law. They had a strong bond. He would often say: We are the only three in this world, woe betide the last one to die."

'"And who was the last one?"

'"My cousin Ida. Carlo died first in '49, then Ludovico in '63. Then Ida died in '72. With them the Trivulzio family died out."'

VIII

From all this it would seem that Carlo Trivulzio was a 'man of honour'. But evidently his concept of honour did not concern itself with the seduction of inexperienced young girls, their almost certain pregnancy and a somewhat hasty method of ridding himself of the inconvenience.

Probably, as Cacciatori, the chief constable of Verona said, Trivulzio did have supper that famous evening with some other officers, but the initiative to make Isolina abort was not his. It is thought that the girl died without the officers meaning it to happen. And one of them, the most enterprising and the most cynical, decided to cut her up in pieces. The possibility cannot be excluded that this was the medical officer who was talked about more than once at the Todeschini trial, without his ever being named. The fact is that all the experts were agreed on one thing: the body was cut up in sections by an 'expert' hand.

Trivulzio's silence was probably owing to his sense of honour, his proverbial coldness, his courage and his deep attachment to the army.

Had he told how it all happened he would have exonerated himself from the more serious accusations, but would have compromised others, making it impossible for the Alpini to keep out of the 'filthy business', as the newspapers called it.

A group of officers implicated in a clandestine abortion (what's more in a restaurant and almost as a joke, using a fork), let alone in a collective murder – even if it were not meant to happen – and the subsequent cutting up and disposal of the body would have seriously damaged the Alpini's image just at a time when the government was attaching great importance to its military prestige.

We can say then that Trivulzio acted the hero. Exactly that kind of heroism is required by war: sacrificing oneself for the group, for the collective (in this case for a class), for one's country.

Had Trivulzio said Yes, I made Isolina pregnant, but then someone else murdered her and cut her up into pieces, he would unquestionably have got a few years' imprisonment, but he would also have involved the army in a scandalous and degrading trial.

By keeping quiet he gave the judges the possibility of passing a vague and nebulous sentence; he gave the army a chance to save its face; he gave his comrades the possibility of continuing their careers. In short, he sacrificed himself out of his love for the army. The eighth regiment of the Alpini (and behind them the entire army and the Ministry of Domestic Affairs) thanked him for it by protecting him from the socialists who wanted the truth 'at all costs'; from the members of Isolina's family; from the journalists (who in reality were almost all pro-government and therefore easy to persuade); and by making him first a colonel and then a general.

But something must have stuck in Carlo Trivulzio's throat: the unspoken truth, that he alone had to pay excessively for a crime which was committed by the group; for his complicity which turned into a lifetime's conspiracy of silence; and for the burden of an ambiguous judgement against him which he shouldered till his death.

All this, together with his much praised 'sense of honour', probably inspired in him a need to expiate, which made him run off to faraway places, never to marry, to shut himself up in his house and to die stoically as his stomach cancer devoured him.

His kind of death was a symbolic reminder of Isolina's suffering. The womb of a nineteen-year-old girl sheltering a baby was profaned and destroyed. And so he, the officer who was responsible, if only indirectly, for that death, was gripped by an illness which destroyed him there, in his stomach, the symbolic site of procreation and nourishment.

PART THREE

The Todeschini Trial

I

In November 1901, Carlo Trivulzio finally began proceedings against Todeschini, as the latter had publicly hoped for months and for which end he had pursued Trivulzio with provocative articles.

Soon afterwards the innkeeper Annibale Isotta brought an action against *Verona del Popolo* and Todeschini wrote: 'For us, such actions are like so many wedding invitations. They will enable us to bring the facts to light and reveal to the public the results of the investigations we have been conducting over the last ten months.'

On 9 November the trial opened. 'In our Court today,' *Il Gazzettino* wrote, 'presided over by Cavalier Salvadori, that famous and fearless magistrate, the trial opens against the socialist deputy Mario Todeschini, editor-in-chief of *Verona del Popolo*, who is being sued for defamation of character by Lieutenant Trivulzio because of his articles about the woman who was cut up in pieces.

'The public is keenly interested in this lawsuit; it is waiting impatiently for it to begin and will follow its unfolding with passionate curiosity.

'This curiosity is well founded, when it is considered that the lawsuit is linked to the mystery which has shrouded the disappearance of Isolina Canuti, whose mortal remains, it is thought, were identified in the pieces of a body retrieved from the fast-moving waters of the Adige.

'Our readers certainly remember the enquiries we made to disentangle the twisted thread of this terrible plot. We reported every circumstance, no matter how tenuous, which might bring those guilty to justice.

'Lieutenant Trivulzio, who was Isolina Canuti's lover, was arrested. Public opinion was aroused. Extremely serious accusations were made against various people. But the mysterious tangle could not be unravelled. Everything vanished like a soap bubble.'

At this point the newspapers clearly took sides: *Il Gazzettino* and *Verona del Popolo* were for Isolina, *L'Arena*, *L'Adige*, *Verona Fedele*, *Resto del Carlino*, *L'Altra* for the other side. The *Corriere della Sera* sat on the fence, sometimes taking an interest in discovering the truth, at other times attacking evidence that produced anti-Trivulzio revelations.

Verona del Popolo started off triumphantly, writing about 'A lawsuit against the military'. And here it made a mistake because it put the other newspapers in a position where they had to treat the debate as a political rather than a criminal one. Once again Isolina was forgotten in a fight of national proportions for and against the army.

L'Arena suddenly began defensive manoeuvres with a summary, partisan in tone: 'At number 25, Corso Cavour, lives the family of an employee of the large Tressa administration. It is the family of Felice Canuti. The head of the family, a gentle, good, honest man, had a daughter, Isolina, aged 19, who was a disgrace to him. Extremely libidinous and lascivious, she made boyfriends in the 3rd and 4th Alpini with a curious ease and her greatest torment was not to enjoy sufficient freedom to abandon herself to her unbridled passions. . . .

'She was not beautiful – a little lop-sided about the shoulders, of medium height, highly strung – yet she was lively and had an appetite for life. She was fond of a girlfriend named Emma Poli who lived in a cramped working-class district and was either a schoolteacher, or in the process of becoming one. Recently Isolina had begun a relationship, not a platonic one, to say the least, with a Lieutenant Trivulzio who had rented a room from them in their house. After a few months she realized that she was pregnant. But was the lieutenant the father of the child?

'The accusation against Lieutenant Trivulzio is a terrifying one: he is in fact accused of murder, for intending to kill and achieving the death of his lover Isolina Canuti, aged 19. . . . But who can really believe that Trivulzio is the perpetrator of Isolina's violent death? A man who is such a gentle soul, so honest, good and proud! A man who, despite everything, is almost certainly not the child's father . . . none of his friends believes he is guilty. And it was noted how calmly he reacted to Isolina's disappearance and how happily he took part in the masked ball the other night. We most sincerely hope and fervently wish that Lieutenant Trivulzio will be able to prove his complete innocence, and we also wish for his regiment that its good, brave, courageous officer may soon be able to return to his company, restored to the affection of his colleagues and superiors, an affection which moves us profoundly.

'In the courtroom, as throughout the city, there is an extraordinary nervous tension. Everyone runs here and there hunting down entrance tickets, which have become extremely scarce, because the room where the hearing will take place is much too narrow. The crowd throngs the doorway, waits an hour for the opening. Hundreds and hundreds of people congregate in a space twelve metres square.

'Lieutenant Trivulzio has been in the hall since nine o'clock. Young, with a slender figure and with an open, likeable appearance, he has a confident air. He wears the Alpini uniform. . . .

'The lawyers are crowded together. On Todeschini's side: Sarfatti, Musatti, Caperle and Borciani. On Trivulzio's side: Paroli, Pagani-Cesa, Trabucchi, Tassistro. Carlo Pellegrini presides, substituted at the last minute for Cavalier Salvadori. Supporting judges: Giulio Ceccato and Fermo Arfini. State Prosecutor: Masotti. Clerk of the Court: Floriani.

'The honourable Mario Todeschini, the accused, entered the courtroom punctually, with his usual bold and confident air. First of all he asked through his lawyers that the proceedings of the preliminary investigation, from which Trivulzio was acquitted for lack of proof, be brought to public notice and into the hearing.

But the court refused. For if this had been done it would have been difficult for the lawyers to compare the previous testimonies of the witnesses with what they might say now. In fact, in the two years that had passed since Isolina's death many people had changed their opinions, backed out, or said that they 'no longer remember'.

II

During this period of history photographic equipment was awkward and difficult to move. So they used an artist in the courtroom.

The artist at the Todeschini trial was very well known in the city. He was the painter Angelo Dall'Oca Bianca who, seated to one side, gradually sketched portraits of the witnesses, which were then submitted to the judges.

Except for Isolina, of whom we do not even have a family portrait, Dall'Oca Bianca caught on paper the faces, the poses, the expressions of all those who took part in the trial.

First of all, Carlo Trivulzio: tall, slender, with a roundish neck and fingers, an evident desire for calm, nourishment, reassurance. A large face, a beautiful smooth oval, eyes set far apart, brown and sensual. A large protruding mole, round and pronounced, between the nose and mouth, almost a sign of uncontrollable disorder in the middle of a geometrically balanced face.

And then there is Mario Todeschini, his moustaches dashingly turned up, a dark beard covering his chin and cheeks, a sharp nose, a broad and relaxed forehead. Dressed in black, wearing a drooping bow-tie. His face is animated by a pugnacious and courageous expression, but also a deep and inconsolable despair, as if he were at any moment about to ask what purpose there really is to life.

Felice Canuti looks, in Dall'Oca Bianca's little pen portrait, like a rabbi, his neck thin and scrawny, sticking out from a dark greatcoat, his beard thick and severe, a curved nose, thick glasses, a black hat pulled down over his forehead.

Maria Policante: a face young but worn, a fleshy nose, subtly curved lips, elongated eyes sunk in their sockets, hair pulled back and then allowed to fall down again like a fountain covering her forehead, an overcoat with a fur collar, which makes her look fat and awkward.

Clelia Canuti looks as she does on the page of *Il Gazzettino*, as if she were appearing at the window of an inn on an unknown road. She has the snub-nose of the Canutis, poorly shaped small eyes, little well-formed ears, hair bunched at the neck, a tiny mouth with an upper lip which juts over the lower. The end result makes her look like a perpetually surprised Mary Poppins; a stiff little hat decorated with a bow is perched on her head like a saucepan. Her pose is eloquent: she leans forward, with her neck outstretched and her mouth open like a frightened child, trying to remember properly the words of her interrogator.

After the first two interrogations, during which the crowd thronged around the doors, the judges decided to move the hearing to a bigger courtroom. 'Here members of the public who are continuing to pour in in huge numbers find a place to sit, the journalists from the most important Italian newspapers have space in which to write, the large numbers of witnesses take their turn amongst the curious public.'

The hall of the Court of Assizes is 'as spacious as a square and rich in elegant architecture, decoration, friezes. Abundant light filters through five arched windows on one side and three on the other. It is cold. The Court of Appeal, which has allowed the hall to be used, has not provided a means of heating it.'

The hearing 'starts very promptly. At nine-thirty exactly the proceedings begin.'

Trivulzio was the first to be interrogated. His tone was immediately self-confident and arrogant.

III

President: When did you go to live at the Canuti house?

Trivulzio: On the 15th of September in 1899.

Pres.: What opinion did you have of the Canuti family?

Trivulzio: At the beginning I had no relationship with them at all. Later on I exchanged a few words with the young lady. Then she started to come into my room to talk to me about intimate things, about her lovers . . . I said to myself: this girl's a bit loose, she's there for the taking. The young lady hung around me and I had her. That was the only idiotic thing I did.

Pres.: When did this happen?

Trivulzio: On the 27th of October.

Pres.: How long did your house-arrest last? (Trivulzio had been arrested because he had slapped some boys who were making fun of him.) And how long did your relationship with Isolina last?

Trivulzio: The eight days that I was under arrest. Naturally I had nothing to do. I was stretched out on the bed reading D'Annunzio. When the house-arrest ended I left. I had no further need of her.

Caperle: Were you arrested again?

Trivulzio: Yes sir, and so what? (*Murmuring in the courtroom*)

Caperle: Your intimacy with Isolina continued outside the house too? Did you ever go to a trattoria with her?

Trivulzio: No, never. Only once I met her in the Piazza Bra.

Caperle: When did you learn of Isolina's pregnancy?

Trivulzio: In November.

Pres.: What other facts can you tell us?

Trivulzio: At my quarters one day I received a note full of reproaches from the Canuti girl. Another day Clelia Canuti came to beg me to go to the house. I went there and Isolina, who was with the Policante woman, chided me for neglecting her. She added that she was pregnant and that the child was mine. I replied: How can you say such a thing when we were only together for a few days? I knew that she had other lovers, how could I accept that I was the father? Then she began to moan about money to me and tell me that things were going badly, that if her father knew about the business he would kill her. I know that he told her off and beat her for her behaviour. I said to her: If I can be of any use I'll help you rather than see you out on the street. Perhaps you need a change of air.

It was on that occasion that she showed me the powder on the table and said to me, I'm taking that stuff to see if it will get rid of it. I think she also may have added, But it's doing nothing for me.

I returned to my quarters. Nine days later Policante wrote me a letter to beg me to call at the house between eight and nine. The note had the signature 'Maria'. There are so many Marias and I didn't know which one had written. It was Policante though, and that evening she said she had come to me on behalf of Canuti to ask if I could help her to buy a pair of shoes because hers were broken . . . I gave her 10 lire.

Another time I saw her, she told me that she had to leave home because otherwise her father would kill her and she asked me again for help. I gave it to her. After that I saw her a few times. On January 5th she disappeared from home. I found out about it from a soldier and from her father. On the evening of the last day she was at home, he was calm and hopeful that she would come back. I didn't make much of her disappearance: I knew that Isolina had other lovers. . . .

Her father let me see a little book with notes in it written by Isolina. Amongst other things it said, Today, the first of November, my period has not come. Her poor father cried. To comfort him I said: If she has run away she will come back, don't worry. What ideas are you filling your head with? She will be all right!

This is what I said to him and these remarks were repeated to *Verona del Popolo*, which interpreted them differently. Then one evening, on the 17th or the 18th, I can't remember, my orderly came and told me that they had found pieces of a human being in the Adige, and that there was a piece of red material. He added, Actually your mistress had a red dress. I advised him to go to the police station immediately. A little while later, I was arrested.

Caperle: Without being interrogated?

Trivulzio: On the 22nd I had an interview which made me very tired. They put so many pieces of evidence in front of me. Her father said one thing, Policante another, and Clelia yet another. I did not understand anything. It was then that I wrote that letter to my colonel which was interpreted as a confession. But you would have to have it in for me to see that as a confession.

Pres.: What is your opinion of all this?

Trivulzio: In my opinion someone used my name when they were trying to get an abortion in order to lend some respectability to the thing.

Caperle: Could you tell us which officers used to go to the Chiodo Restaurant?

Trivulzio: There were those who went there to eat and those who went there for the Society. (The Chiodo Society drew together soldiers who had also composed their own Chiodo song, the words of which went: Down in a little lane/Where Annibale's getting fat/You'll find the Chiodo* temple/And the mighty Chiodo race!/We'll use our might!/For an honest fight!)

Pres.: Did you take women to the Society?

Trivulzio: No, women, gambling and politics were banned.

Caperle: But do you not know that on the 14th two women were taken there by the officers?

Trivulzio: I don't believe that. But in any event that evening I did not go to the Chiodo.

Caperle: After Isolina disappeared did you not send her father 25 lire?

Trivulzio: No, no. After January 5th I knew nothing more about her.

Sarfatti: What theories did you have about the way in which the cutting up of Isolina happened?

Trivulzio: I haven't managed to form an opinion.

Sarfatti: Did you not make enquiries yourself, to find out what had happened, and also because you had been asked to by her father?

Trivulzio: The police were looking for her – why should I do what the police were doing?

*Chiodo: lit., a nail

Sarfatti: Perhaps out of curiosity to know where a lover of yours had ended up.

Trivulzio: The thought never occurred to me.

P.M.: When you told your orderly to go to the police station to voice his suspicions about Isolina, did he go there?

Trivulzio: My orderly went to her father, and his response was: It's not her.

Sarfatti: Did you know Emma Poli?

Trivulzio: I never knew her. I may have seen her because her father has the luggage shop under the Canuti house.

P.M.: Did you know that she had an officer for a lover?

Trivulzio: I've just found out about it.

Pres.: What did her father say to you?

Trivulzio: He disclosed certain things that his daughter had said. Namely, that she and Isolina had been together with their boyfriends, who had beaten them, and she had succeeded in running away.

Sarfatti: Why is the Poli girl dead?

Trivulzio: It's known that she died in hospital after an unsuccessful labour.

Sarfatti: Did the judge show you some bags stamped with the military emblem?

Trivulzio: They did show me three bags, which they said they found in my house. I said that I had no idea what they were, except for a little leather one which I used to carry to sleep on when I went to the mountains.

Caperle: Were you shown the bags in which Isolina's remains were found?

Trivulzio: No, never.

P.M.: In the first interrogation, what were the pieces of evidence the judge presented to you?

Trivulzio: That her father, for example, told him that I had advised him to make enquiries, and that I had ruined his daughter.

Sarfatti: Do you know Friedman?

Trivulzio: I did not even know that she had been arrested.

Sarfatti: The fact remains that the examining judge made sure that he called her in when the new disclosures concerning De

Mori were made. Did they make you and the witnesses confront one another?

Trivulzio: When I was arrested, yes, there was a confrontation between me and the witnesses, the Canutis and Policante.

Sarfatti: What was the business with Policante about?

Trivulzio: Policante maintained that I had said that for a certain sum of money you could have a man murdered.

Sarfatti: But the conclusion was that she maintained that you had encouraged Isolina to have an abortion?

Trivulzio: She did. She was referring to something that I might have said lightly, just between ourselves.

Sarfatti: When the new fact emerged, that the midwife De Mori had been offered 300 lire in Policante's name to undertake a criminal act for Isolina, were you interrogated by the examining magistrate?

Trivulzio: No, I was no longer considered under accusation.

Caperle: Do you know that letters were sent to Policante from Conegliano, a place where an Alpini regiment was stationed, letters which offered her money to buy her silence?

Trivulzio: I never heard about that. What letters are they?

Caperle: They have been deposited as evidence. They are anonymous letters.

Trivulzio: Ah!

Pres.: You do realize that your letter to the colonel sounds like a confession. . . .

Trivulzio: It is a letter which I would write even now, with all its mistakes . . . so many things had lowered my morale, I was embattled on so many fronts that I thought I would lose my mind.

Sarfatti: Lieutenant Trivulzio, did you not think of advising Isolina against taking the powder?

Trivulzio: I thought it was one of her usual lies. I didn't attach much weight to it.

Caperle: Do you know the Policante woman?

Trivulzio: I knew that she had lovers. Isolina told me that too.

P.M.: Did you frequent the Trattoria Chiodo?

Trivulzio: I'll make a distinction: I used to go to the Chiodo Society and not the trattoria.

Caperle: But they were in the same building.

Sarfatti: On the evening of the 14th, that of the crime, were you at the Chiodo?

Trivulzio: No, I was at the theatre.

Pres.: Because in your letter to your colonel you said that you were implicated in a crime. . . .

Trivulzio: I was at the Scalzi for something on there.

Sarfatti: You sent the War Ministry a memorandum. What did it contain?

Trivulzio: The results of the enquiries which I had been making.

Sarfatti: What would those enquiries be?

Trivulzio: The result of the investigations was almost nothing. Naturally if others could shed no light what could I do? I was convinced that Policante was a fine rogue, very capable of participating in the crime and saying that a lieutenant was involved in order to get the responsibility off her back.

P.M.: How is it that you never took an action against Policante?

Trivulzio: In order to prove defamation you have to find witnesses.

Pres.: But her false testimony was in the proceedings.

Trivulzio: I told the judge it was false.

Caperle: But you took no action.

Trivulzio: Much later I heard that she was continuing to spread rumours and I looked for witnesses.

Caperle: And did you take out an action?

Trivulzio: I denounced her for calumny.

Caperle: For calumny or falsehood?

Trivulzio: I don't know the legal terms. I denounced her.

Pres.: Did Policante have any reason to be against you?

Trivulzio: No.

Pres.: And why should she have an ulterior motive?

Trivulzio: I am convinced that she got involved in this affair for some reason.

Sarfatti: Did the examining magistrate question her about her participation in getting an abortion and in the cutting up of the body?

Trivulzio: I don't think so.

Caperle: On the evening of your release you went to the
Chiodo where a toast was drunk to you?
Trivulzio: Yes, sir.
Caperle: And the Chiodo song was sung?
Trivulzio: Very loudly.
Sarfatti: Has the lieutenant seen the rough copy of the re-
proachful note sent to him by Isolina?
Trivulzio: The examining judge showed it to me.
Sarfatti: That letter would be a valuable asset in this case.
Caperle: So valuable that the lieutenant tore it up as soon as he
got hold of it.

So ended Trivulzio's first long interrogation. He was then
called again to reply, but only briefly. The curious thing was
that Trivulzio admitted everything except his direct responsibility: he did not deny that he made love to Isolina, he did not
deny that he knew she was pregnant (and the little red book,
which was never shown to the judges and which he himself
quoted, mentioned that the pregnancy began on the first of
November). He stated only that he had nothing to do with the
conception. He did not deny that he talked to Isolina about the
powder to bring on an abortion, but he made nothing of it.
Finally, he came to admit that he had advised a 'change of air'.
He said that he gave Isolina 25 lire (which was a big enough
sum then, given that Trivulzio paid his orderly 5 lire a month)
but only 'as charity'.

All in all Clelia's testimony was never denied. And Clelia was
Trivulzio's most important accuser. But he never thought of
bringing an action against her.

IV

'Clelia Canuti is a frail, wan young girl. She is 17 but looks 14',
wrote the *Corriere della Sera*. 'She is small, thin, her head is
disproportionately large for her body and she has the beginning

of a goitre', continued *Il Gazzettino*. 'She is cleanly dressed and speaks in a nasal voice in Venetian dialect.'

Pres.: What do you know about the lieutenant?
Clelia: I know that Isolina went to her room with him.
Pres.: And what did she tell you?
Clelia: That once the lieutenant had given her 50 lire. But she only let me see 25 of it.
Pres.: And why did he give her the money?
Clelia: She told me it was to buy a powder because she was pregnant and wanted to recover.
Pres.: And then?
Clelia: She showed me the powder; it was white. She said that she got it from an ugly old woman.
Pres.: And did she tell you anything else?
Clelia: Yes, that if the powder was no good the lieutenant would send her to Milan because there were good women there who could get rid of it.
Pres.: And did she say she would go?
Clelia: She started to cry because she didn't want to have an abortion.
Pres.: Go on.
Clelia: Another time she said she had 10 lire to buy a powder.
Pres.: Do you know anything else?
Clelia: One night we went out with Isolina and we met a lieutenant in the artillery, Nineci, and then a medical doctor. (*Hilarity in the courtroom*)
Pres.: You mean a medical lieutenant.
Clelia: Yes. Ines Bonomelli followed us and came along. When we got home the lieutenant caressed Isolina a lot but she wasn't interested. I heard her say secretly to Ines, I brought this lieutenant here for you. The lieutenant then took Isolina to his house in Via Pallone. He caressed her a lot, he kissed her, but he didn't get anywhere. He kept saying to her, Give me a kiss, give me a kiss. When he tried to pick her up, Isolina said If you leave me alone I'll give you a kiss.
Pres.: And did she give him one?
Clelia: Yes.

Pres.: And afterwards you went home?

Clelia: Yes. Isolina told me that she didn't like the lieutenant.

Pres.: Did you know about a letter from Isolina to Lieutenant Trivulzio?

Clelia: Isolina read it to me. She told the lieutenant that he had made her pregnant and that she had never had a relationship with the medical lieutenant.

Pagani: And the lieutenant read the four lines of that letter before tearing it up?

Sarfatti: Could we have a rough copy of it?

Pagani: It's been confiscated by the judge.

Sarfatti: Could the Canuti father ask to have it back again? It's something that was taken from his house; we could ask for the famous little red book as well. And Policante could ask for her anonymous letter from Conegliano. (*But neither the letters nor Isolina's diary ever turned up again.*)

Pres.: And what about the business with the bodice?

Clelia: On the second floor of our house there was a seamstress who made women's underclothes. Isolina ordered a bodice from her with lace and bows. The seamstress asked: Is it for daytime or night? For night, for night, Isolina replied. She told me that she would go to bed with her lover in that bodice. One night I heard her get up, put on her slippers and the bodice and go into the lieutenant's room. She told me that she was in bed with the lieutenant until four in the morning.

Pres.: Was that the only time?

Clelia: The only time she stayed until four. She did go at other times though, but I don't know how long she stayed.

Pres.: Did she see Lieutenant Trivulzio often?

Clelia: Once he went and asked for a bottle to buy some marsala for Isolina, who was pregnant. Another time he bought some marzipan sweets for the same reason.

Borciani: Tell the story of the marsala more clearly.

Clelia: This is how it happened: Isolina once told the lieutenant that she'd like some marsala. The lieutenant asked papa for a litre bottle. The bottle came back full up and then Isolina said to me, That bottle is for me and he's given it to me because I'm pregnant.

Borciani: And did Isolina drink the marsala?

Clelia: Me and Isolina, yes.

Pagani: Did you feel ill after that Clelia?

Clelia: No.

Borciani: It had no effect. Do you know the name of the medical lieutenant?

Clelia: No.

Borciani (*to Lieutenant Trivulzio*): And did you know it?

Clelia (*replying for him*): Yes, he knew it.

Trivulzio (*interrupting*): Isolina showed me his letters but I didn't know who it was.

Borciani: Lieutenant, do you remember the business with the marsala?

Trivulzio: I don't remember exactly, but it could very well be.

Borciani: Is it possible that you don't remember his name given that Isolina talked to you about him?

Trivulzio: No.

Pres. (*to Clelia*): What other things did Isolina tell you?

Clelia: One day she said to me: I'm pregnant. Oh, what are you trying to tell me? I asked her. And she told me, I'm talking about the baby in me.

Pres.: Did Trivulzio talk to you?

Clelia: He asked me one day, How old are you? I replied, sixteen. And he said: It's time you had a boyfriend. He'll take care of you . . . and he turned to Isolina, laughing. (*The public stirs and murmurs.*)

Pres.: What did the lieutenant say after the disappearance?

Clelia: One day when I was in the kitchen, the lieutenant said to papa, Signor Canuti, drink up, drink up, don't worry about your daughter, she's safe. Papa didn't hear. Policante, who was in the kitchen, told him soon afterwards.

Pagani: But Clelia, you didn't hear it?

Clelia: No, because I was a little way away from Policante.

Pres.: Think a bit, do you remember anything else?

Clelia: Isolina threatened to hit me, to kill me, to let me die of starvation if ever I told papa what I knew.

Pres.: And you said nothing?

Clelia: I was frightened of her.

Judge: Were you present when the powder was discussed?

Clelia: Isolina talked to me about it.

Pres.: What else did Isolina tell you?

Clelia: She told me a story about a girl who died from having an abortion. She showed me a veil and tried it on. I said it made her look sad and she said: If it makes me look sad all the better. Then I saw her go out and make her way towards the Officers' Club. On the table I saw that she had left 3 lire. I went to pick them up, but my brother told me not to.

Pres.: Did Isolina talk to you any more about her condition?

Clelia: One day she had a bedwarmer in her lap. It was a present ordered by Lieutenant Trivulzio and Isolina said to him, showing her stomach: I've got Trivulzio here, eh, I've got Trivulzio! (*Great agitation in the courtroom*)

Pres.: Did your sister confide in you that she had also known a lieutenant in the Bersaglieri regiment?

Clelia: Her first boyfriend was from the Bersaglieri. He and Isolina came home together and he used to do naughty things. I used to hear Isolina saying, Oh God, that's enough, oh God, that's enough.

Pres.: Did they sleep together?

Clelia: Yes, sir.

Borciani: How long ago did that happen?

Clelia: A long time ago.

P.M.: When did the lieutenant and Isolina begin their relationship?

Clelia: A few days after he came to our house. The lieutenant said, Would Signorina Isolina like to make love with me? Seven or eight days later Isolina went to his room.

Sarfatti: The lieutenant stated formally yesterday that he had sexual relations with Isolina on only two or three occasions during the period when he was under house-arrest.

Trabucchi: It was the Policante woman who ruined Isolina. What do you know about Policante?

Clelia: When we were in Vicolo Disciplina, Policante taught her dirty words.

Pres.: Did you hear them?

Clelia: No, they used to say them in Vicolo Disciplina.

Caperle: And did Policante teach you bad things?
Clelia: Me? No, never.

It is evident that Clelia was sometimes candid to the point of
half-wittedness. A frightened child who was trying to please
the judges, and did not realize the effect of the things she was
saying. She did not even think of protecting her sister.

It would have taken very few words on her part to damn
Trivulzio. But she didn't say them. And this finally showed
only too clearly that the things she did reveal were the truth.

For her this trial was an opportunity to make her presence felt, if
only timidly, showing that she was more mature and confident
than she might have appeared. It was an opportunity to express,
in agreement with the neighbours, her disapproval of her sister,
'the little whore', as she was known in the neighbourhood.

Her replies were a mixture of candour, simple-mindedness,
sibling cruelty, ignorance. There was in Isolina's relatives,
whether her father, Felice Canuti, or Clelia, such a carelessness,
such a lack of self-regard that at times they seemed to be their
own worst enemy.

But behind that carelessness, which was very near to idiocy,
there was not a trace of vulgarity or coarseness. Rather, what
emerged was a bitter incapacity for self-love, tied to a childish
and painful sensitivity. They did not love themselves, those
Canutis. And it seems that Isolina was affected by the same
weakness.

Their lunatic self-neglect is somehow heartbreaking. They
offered themselves up as victims before the blow fell, uncom-
plaining, without expecting any satisfaction, so bereft of vanity
and shrewdness as to appear moving and poetic.

They seemed to be saying that the world, with all its pettiness
and horrors, was no concern of theirs. They left the torturers,
the executioners, the money-lenders, complete freedom to act.
They returned evil with the maddest and rashest generosity,
forgetting themselves, without asking recognition from heaven
or even remembrance on earth.

V

Maria Policante, aged 30, a domestic servant. 'She is pale, thin,
wears a little cloak over her shoulders and is bareheaded.' This
is how *Il Gazzettino* described her. And in the *Corriere della Sera*:
'She is not ugly, and dresses rather ostentatiously, with a kind
of dubious elegance. The public greeted her appearance with a
lively curiosity for which they were reprimanded by the President.'

President: Do you know that Lieutenant Trivulzio used to
make love with Isolina?
Policante: Yes, sir. She said that Lieutenant Trivulzio was
courting her but that she did not like him much. She said that
she had a lieutenant from the Bersaglieri before.
Pres.: And what else?
Policante: She said that they used to go for walks.
Pres.: Do you know about the scandal and the complaints from
the neighbours?
Policante: No, she only told me that the lieutenant was courting her at home and outside.
Pres.: When was the lieutenant in the Bersaglieri transferred?
Policante: I don't know.
Pres.: What did Isolina tell you about her love affairs?
Policante: She said that Lieutenant Trivulzio wanted to take her
to a midwife. She replied that she didn't want to because at
least she could make sure that even if he didn't marry her he
would give her something. One day she invited me to go with
her to a midwife. We went to Friedman who told her bluntly
that she was pregnant.
Judge Ceccato: Did she say how far gone she was?
Policante: A month.
Pres.: Did Isolina confide anything else in you?
Policante: She told me, The lieutenant wants me to go to Milan
but I don't want to. I'll wait until he goes on holiday and then
I'll take a room and he'll pay for it.
Pres.: What did the lieutenant say when he knew what Isolina
had in mind?

Policante: He declared that he didn't want that at all, that he didn't want her to go on being pregnant.

Pres.: Did she get money from the lieutenant?

Policante: One evening Isolina was having an argument with her father and was crying. The lieutenant asked me why she was crying. I replied that she was in a mess and he gave me 10 lire to give to Isolina.

Pres.: Who suggested the midwife De Mori in Vicolo Leoni?

Policante: Isolina. We went there together. She stopped at the doorway and sent me on in front of her to make an offer. The midwife replied: I've had four myself, she can certainly have one!

P.M.: Did the lieutenant want to go with Isolina to the midwife?

Policante: Isolina told me he did, I don't know.

Pres.: Was De Mori consulted on another occasion?

Policante: De Mori asked me if my friend was the mistress of a dark-haired lieutenant. I replied that she wasn't. And I told her that she was Lieutenant Trivulzio's mistress.

Pres.: Did the lieutenant know how Isolina disappeared?

Policante: He swore to me that he knew nothing.

Caperle: The witness said on the 16th of last January that the remains found in the Adige were those of Isolina.

Policante: I said that they were – after having seen the clothes.

Pres.: Do you know if the Chiodo Society allowed in women?

Policante: I don't know.

Pagani: The rules forbid it and fines are imposed.

Caperle: But the fines are glasses of wine which it's possible to enjoy drinking.

Pres.: Did you talk to Lieutenant Trivulzio?

Policante: One evening the lieutenant was up lighting the stove. He told me that he wanted to send Isolina to Milan, that he knew some people there, that he had been involved in similar affairs before and that they had turned out all right. I said, You won't find anyone in Verona. And he said, With money you can find anything.

Sarfatti: Didn't he add anything else?

Policante: He added that if there's someone threatening you, you can find someone to kill him if you've got the money. I told him, it would be better if you told her father everything. And he said No, I don't want this kind of thing, I don't want to bring children into the world. And it's stupid of you to make Isolina more depressed instead of cheering her up.

Caperle: Didn't he talk about spitting on the ground in relation to abortion?

Policante: Yes, he said, It's such a little thing, and right at the beginning, it's just like spitting on the ground.

Borciani: Did you receive anonymous letters, Policante?

Policante: Yes.

Borciani: What did they say?

Policante: They said, Dear Maria, what you said in the police station and the magistrate's court is quite enough, you have said too much. When it's all over you will get a very, very big present. I am well informed by someone who hangs about in the police station that in a few days it will all be over and meanwhile, if you need any money write immediately, poste restante, to Signor Rughi Gaetano in Conegliano.

Borciani: What have you done with the letter?

Policante: I took it to police officer Tedeschi who said they got letters like that every day.

Sarfatti: Have you told the judges everything?

Policante: Yes, everything.

Pagani: However, the first time you didn't mention that you went to De Mori's house.

Policante: I didn't think that it was important.

Todeschini: Lawyer Pagani knows the minutes of the preliminary investigation and we do not. Our position is unequal. I again request information about the interrogations during the preliminary investigation.

(*But the minutes of the hearing of the preliminary investigation never turned up and the lawyers were never able to read them.*)

Sarfatti: When did Isolina tell you she had become pregnant?

Policante: A month after the lieutenant was at their house.

Sarfatti: At their house as a guest, or under arrest?

Policante: A month after he went to live in the house.

(Trivulzio went to live in the Canuti house on 15 September 1899.)

Sarfatti: I remember the statement made by the lieutenant that he read in Isolina's little memo book that on November 1st her period had not come.

Trivulzio: It said precisely: Today, the first of November, my period has not come.

Sarfatti: Therefore, according to your evidence, if in November she was in her first month of pregnancy, in January she was in her third month. . . .

Pres.: Have you seen this little book, Policante?

Policante: No.

Sarfatti: Have you ever had any animosity towards Lieutenant Trivulzio?

Policante: No, there was no reason to.

Pres.: Lieutenant Trivulzio, is it true that you advised Isolina to go to Milan?

Trivulzio: I said it several times but not with any wicked purpose in mind. It was Policante who misconstrued it.

Policante: Me, sir?

Trivulzio: Yes, you. I never went to take her to a midwife!

Borciani: Did you say to Policante, Come here you, you're a woman of judgement, while that one there, she's stupid . . .?

Trivulzio: I never said that.

Policante: Yet I remember it well.

Trivulzio: Where were we, tell me that, where were we?

Policante: In the lieutenant's room.

Trivulzio: What she's saying is untrue. The time she came to me was when I gave her the 10 lire.

(Here the conflict degenerated into a heated argument. The enraged lieutenant insisted on saying that Policante was telling lies, and Policante calmly repeated that it was the truth.)

Sarfatti: Why do you suppose, Lieutenant Trivulzio, that Policante is saying things that are untrue?

Trivulzio: I didn't know Policante. The first time I met her was the day Clelia called me over. On that occasion Isolina told me for the first time that she was pregnant. That she had been to a midwife. That it was Policante who had taken her there. The powder was there on the table.

Borciani: Do you know anything about the powder, Policante?

Policante: I know absolutely nothing about the powder except that Isolina told me the lieutenant had asked her to take it. She declared that if the lieutenant insisted she would say that she had taken it. She would substitute two packets of medicine she had already, which the doctor had prescribed for something else.

Sarfatti (*to Trivulzio*): In your opinion, why would the woman make accusations against you?

Trivulzio: Because it is she who knows everything, that's why she accuses me.

Sarfatti: How can you be so confident that Policante knows everything, given that you know nothing? And if she knows, why would she accuse you if you're innocent?

Borciani: Tell the truth Trivulzio!

Trivulzio: She went with Canuti, she gave her advice, she did everything (*the public makes a noise*). Policante knows everything, she advised her about the abortion, she tried to make her have one.

Borciani: But she couldn't have made her pregnant could she! Why do you accuse her so unfairly?

Policante: It didn't matter to me whether she had an abortion. On the contrary, I told her to keep the baby.

Trivulzio: But you took her to the midwife.

Policante: Isolina asked me to do that, so I did it. I know that she wanted the two of us to go together because the midwife, seeing two poor women without any money, would say no, whereas if we had gone with the lieutenant, she might have agreed.

Pagani: How many times did you see the lieutenant, Policante?

Policante: It must have been three or four times. I went to the house because I couldn't believe the things that Isolina was telling me about the lieutenant.

Pagani: Do you know about a letter written to the lieutenant with the signature 'Maria'?

Policante: I don't know anything about it, I don't know how to write.

Trabucchi: How long did Policante work for the Canuti family?

(*It was significant that Trabucchi asked this question at this point. Trivulzio was in a corner and the attention of the Court and the public had to be diverted from him towards facts that would catch people's imagination and show the witness in a bad light.*)

Policante: I was there twice, once for a period of two years.
Trabucchi: Did you have a habit of going around the house naked during the summer, Policante?
Policante: No, never.
Sarfatti: I object to that kind of question!

(*The session was interrupted for an hour. Trivulzio was accompanied to his house by a menacing crowd, and it was so large that next day Sarfatti felt it his responsibility to call on the public to have respect for the person who was bringing the action. The lawyer Trabucchi took up the case, again, using various tactics to divert attention.*)

Trabucchi: Is it true that when Policante was a servant at the Canuti house, her behaviour was so scandalous that the neighbours had to complain? Is it true that she led Isolina into prostitution? Is it true that she lured passers-by and enticed them into the Canuti house?
Sarfatti: It seems to me quite incredible that you are asking the witness all these disgusting questions. The witnesses are not here to be submitted to this torture.

Lawyer Trabucchi is getting his questions inscribed in the records, and understands the conclusions that will be drawn from them. They will remain in the public memory and that of the court. The character of the witness will be blackened, even if there is no truth to the claims.

Pagani: Until when did you see Isolina?
Policante: Until the 5th, at midday.
Pagani: Where was she?
Policante: I saw her in the piazza. She told me she was going

home to take some money that she had to give to her father. We went back and forth between the cheese shop and other places. She bought some sweet mustard and gave me some of it. That day she seemed very reserved. When she left me she said, If you don't see me I'll be at home this evening.

P.M.: What did you talk about during those last few days?

Policante: She no longer talked to me about trying to get an abortion. Instead she was saying that she wanted to get a room to rent and take her stuff there.

P.M.: On the evening of the 5th, did you go to Isolina's house?

Policante: No, as I was going home I heard that old Canuti had been there looking for his daughter. It had happened on other occasions because sometimes when Isolina was away from home she told her father that she was going to my house.

P.M.: What did Canuti say to you?

Policante: That if anyone asked me where Isolina was I should say that she had gone to the country; he didn't want anyone to know about her running away.

Pres.: Did he ask the lieutenant for news about Isolina?

Policante: Yes, but he said that he didn't know anything. I asked, If he doesn't know, who does?

P.M.: Are you convinced that no one but he knew where Isolina was?

Policante: He was her lover so he should know.

VI

On 15 November it was Felice Canuti's turn. He was described by the *Corriere della Sera* as being 'hard of hearing and not in the least intelligent'. But as we shall see, he was a tragic figure. Just like Clelia, he was not very aware of what he should or might say to help Isolina. Like Clelia, he did not think of making accusations against Trivulzio, even though he did so unintentionally.

He appeared to be consumed with a single violent feeling:

the love for his daughter Isolina compared with which the gossip, the spiteful murmurings of neighbours and friends were like the squabbling of so many birds of prey up in the trees. He tried to shoo them away with impetuous gestures, like a mad and melancholy Don Quixote.

Pres.: Tell us what you know concerning your daughter Isolina.

Canuti: The lieutenant used to come and see me often after the 5th of January, saying again and again: I'm sorry, old man, but be brave. Then one Sunday I went to him and said, But the 25 lire that I saw in my daughter's hand will run out! And he replied: Whoever gave her those will give her some more.

Pres.: And didn't he say that Isolina would come back?

Canuti: He said to me more than once, Don't worry, she will come back.

Pres.: Didn't he talk about some safe place?

Canuti: If I remember properly he said, Don't worry, don't worry, she is in a safe place.

Pres.: Did it seem to you that the lieutenant knew where Isolina was?

Canuti: He was saying it either to comfort me or for some other reason, you can understand that I don't know which.

Pres.: But didn't you have suspicions of any kind?

Canuti: After the lieutenant was arrested I suspected something and said to my children, It looks like he knew something.

Pres.: Why?

Canuti: Because when someone says, Don't worry, don't worry, they must know something.

Sarfatti: Did you, Canuti, talk to Trivulzio's orderly after the remains were discovered?

Canuti: Yes. He said to me, Don't worry Signor, that could never be your daughter.

Pres.: When did you learn about Isolina's relationship with the lieutenant?

Canuti: I learnt about it from my daughter Clelia. She told me that Isolina was flirting and that she got pregnant.

Pres.: Did you ever tell Isolina off about her behaviour?

Canuti: The neighbours were complaining and I told Isolina about it. She'd reply, Don't worry, don't worry. I can't say what she did because I was busy from nine in the morning until five in the afternoon.

Borciani: Did Clelia tell you about the powder?

Canuti: She told me that Isolina had taken a powder to bring on an abortion.

P.M.: Did she say Isolina had taken the powder at the lieutenant's suggestion?

Canuti: I think so, but I don't remember very well.

Judge Ceccato: Was a little notebook belonging to Isolina found?

Canuti: I found a little notebook in which there were notes that I took to be scribbling, amongst a lot of love letters from a lieutenant in the Bersaglieri regiment, who went to Ancona, and from a lieutenant who was a medic. I went to ask the lieutenant to explain her scribblings and he calmed me down by saying that these were the dates of her periods.

Pres.: What was Isolina like? Large, fat, well developed?

Canuti: A little taller than Clelia, there.

Judge Ceccato: And did she have any defects?

Canuti: Her neck always hurt and she had eczema and scars on her face and hands.

Clelia (*interrupting*): And a bone stuck out behind. It came after she had whooping cough.

Canuti: For pity's sake let me go, I have to go to work. Ah, if only Clelia had told me, if only she had told me, nothing would have happened . . . and if the lieutenant had said something to me then it would not have happened as it did.

Pres.: Did you find anything else of Isolina's in the house?

Canuti: In a cupboard I found a fustian bodice, embroidered all over, which Isolina had hidden. That made an impression on me.

Pres.: Why?

Canuti: Because Clelia told me that Isolina wore it when she went to bed with Lieutenant Trivulzio.

Borciani: Did you show it to the lieutenant?

Canuti: Yes, and he said, That's a tart's stuff!

Judge Arfini: What kind of a bodice was it, did it go over or under?

Canuti: Ask Clelia, she knows all about that kind of thing.

Pres.: How did you learn about Isolina's disappearance?

Canuti: When I returned home at five o'clock I couldn't find her. I looked in all her friends' houses everywhere, but I couldn't find her.

Pres.: Did it seem to you that Policante knew something about her disappearance?

Canuti: My dear, Policante, Ines Bonomelli, Poli and Gisella Donarche were the only ones who could know.

Pres.: But what did Policante say on the evening of the 5th?

Canuti: She said, Wherever you think she's gone, she'll be back, she'll be back.

Pres.: Did Gisella give you any clue?

Canuti: I went round to her one morning and found her in a bed which was big enough for three people. She assured me that she knew nothing.

Borciani: Why should these girls know where Isolina was?

Canuti: Because they were her friends, because she confided in them.

Judge Ceccato: This relationship of Isolina's with the medical lieutenant, was it a new one?

Canuti: Clelia might know about that.

Sarfatti: And her relationship with the lieutenant from the Bersaglieri regiment?

Canuti: I learned about him from Isolina herself after he had gone away, because she kept on repeating to me: He was my beautiful man, my beauty! And I asked her, Who was this beauty then?

Pres.: Why did you dismiss Policante, and what do you think of her?

Canuti: I sent her away because people were saying that it was bad for Isolina to associate with her.

P.M.: But didn't you see for yourself how Policante behaved?

Canuti: I saw nothing because I was at the office all day. And then I only saw things through my daughter Isolina's eyes – she was my idol. I told her that people were complaining and she replied, Those people don't like me. And I believed her. Let me go – I can't bear it anymore. . . .

After saying this Canuti was allowed to step down and was not questioned further.

VII

A series of important witnesses followed. The first: Alessandro Carlini, a law student aged 23, and a former editor at the *Gazzettino di Verona*. Carlini said he knew the Canuti family. 'It was my mother who got Isolina into the Pericolanti school when her mother was dying.' Her father later took her away from there because he suspected that her crooked spine was the result of her living in that draughty atmosphere.

When Carlini heard about Isolina, he went to see Clelia, and she told him about the powder which Trivulzio had given her sister. 'I took it but nothing happened.' To which Trivulzio had replied, 'You will have to give birth in Milan or have an abortion in Verona.'

Clelia also told him about the 25 lire that Trivulzio had given her sister to buy the powder to bring on an abortion. And how Trivulzio had comforted her father, telling him, 'Don't worry, Signor Felice, Isolina is in a safe place.'

Carlini wrote down every detail in a notebook and showed it to the editor of the newspaper. The editor then sent him off to make further enquiries. De Mori's name had only just come up. So Carlini turned up at the midwife's house and, after an initial refusal, she told him everything.

'One day Maria Policante came to my house asking if I would carry out an abortion for some girl. She added, The person who wants to know is an officer in the Alpini.' De Mori then confided in a friend and the friend said, 'It would be a pleasure – try and find out who the officer is!' De Mori met Policante one day and asked her. 'Do me a favour and don't say a word: the man concerned is Lieutenant Trivulzio.'

De Mori, in order not to forget the name, wrote it on the wall as soon as she was home, but since she had heard it as 'Tribulzio' instead of Trivulzio she wrote it with a 'b' instead of with a 'v'. Then when she heard about his arrest she wiped the name off the wall.

Carlini, like any good journalist, continued his investigations for his own satisfaction. But he maintained his relationship with the police. One day he invited two inspectors from the police to the newspaper's office, 'Bacchetti and Dallari, who confirm facts which I had found out for myself about De Mori'.

At this point the situation begins to sound like something out of a detective novel. 'As I didn't trust them, I shut a friend from the editorial staff in a cupboard so that he could hear everything that Bacchetti and Dallari said to me. My friend's name is Barbarani and he can confirm everything I tell you.'

On that occasion the two policemen told him that they had seen the name Trivulzio with their own eyes written on De Mori's wall. But later, when they were interrogated, they denied everything.

He went with another friend, a schoolteacher called Nimini, to find Benedetto Poli, the father of Emma Poli, who had been Isolina's friend and had died in hospital in mysterious circumstances.

Poli told them that he had made three reports to the police station about his daughter's revelations on her deathbed that she had been poisoned. But they had taken no notice of his reports at the police station.

'The people I'm making accusations against have guns and can kill me. But I do want revenge,' the frightened Poli told them.

After Carlini, Dallari was called to give evidence. He was a police officer who at the trial said first one thing and then another and then backed out, initially appearing to want to clarify things and later to keep his mouth shut.

Dallari was amongst the first to carry out investigations on behalf of the Verona police in January 1900.

The president asked him if it was true that he questioned De Mori. And he replied, 'Yes, I called her in. She confirmed that

Policante had been to her to ask for help in carrying out an abortion on a young woman, saying that it involved Lieutenant Trivulzio. I put her statement on record, which I read out to the present chief constable, Officer Tedeschi.'

As for the famous powder for the abortion, 'I sent the guard Bertolini', said Dallari, 'to the Canutis' house, and he reported that a powder was found in the pocket of a dress. I had it analysed and it turned out to contain two kinds of salt, quinine salt and another one. They tell me that if the stuff were taken in large quantities the powder could bring on an abortion.'

There was a certain unwillingness on the part of the judges to go further with the questioning of this representative from the police, and after a little cross-questioning he was sent off.

The midwife De Mori was called. She confirmed that Policante had gone to her on some lieutenant's behalf: 'Is the lieutenant's name Moretti? I asked Policante, and she said No, he is called Trivulzio. As soon as I got home I wrote the name on the wall in the entrance hall so that I would not forget it. I then went to the cobbler's and said to him, How about that, the girl's lover is Lieutenant Trivulzio!'

The only thing she denied was that they discussed money. Dallari talked about 300 lire, which was then a very large sum. De Mori said that that wasn't true. 'I saw it published in *L'Adige* that they had offered me 50 lire. Then they told me that this was a joke, but that joke cost me 3 or 4 lire a day.'

However she refused to carry out the abortion. 'I've already had four children, so she can have one!'

VIII

On 16 November, the former chief constable Cacciatori was called to give evidence. It is worth reporting his interrogation, at least the salient parts.

Pres.: What conclusion did you come to?

Cacciatori: That Lieutenant Trivulzio had something to do with this business.

Pres.: What is your interpretation of what happened?

Cacciatori: The way I see it is this: When the lieutenant learned about the pregnancy, he tried to cut it short. The abortion had lethal effects. He then found himself faced with a corpse. In order to get out of trouble he tried to get rid of the body. (*This caused a sensation in the room. The public was in uproar.*)

Judge Ceccato: Did you get an anonymous letter from Conegliano?

Cacciatori: Yes, and I then took the step of sending a letter poste restante to Lunghi Gaetano's address, which was where the letter had been posted. After a while I was told that the exercise had been futile.

Pagani: What is your opinion of Policante?

Cacciatori: Policante was a woman who easily fell in love, but the facts don't show her in a bad light, and I haven't been able to persuade myself that she acted out of hate or retaliation.

Pagani: Did Policante tell you that she had been to get the powder?

Cacciatori: I think she said that she had been to the midwife with Isolina in order to find out what Isolina's condition was. On the first night, though, she refused to answer questions and I was undecided as to whether to arrest her.

Borciani: Did you ever change your opinion about Lieutenant Trivulzio?

Cacciatori: No, because I never lost my strong suspicions about him.

P.M.: Did you hear people mention any other lieutenant?

Cacciatori: Before I settled on Lieutenant Trivulzio, I investigated Petrini, the lieutenant in the Bersaglieri regiment. But after he left he didn't come back to Verona, nor did Isolina ever go to him.

Pagani: And did you hear about a medical lieutenant?

Cacciatori: I think he was a lieutenant from the hospital. (*Was this the Zamboni whom Emma Poli's father confused with Cavalier Zamboni?*)

Judge Ceccato: Did the manner in which the body was mutilated strike you in any way?

Cacciatori: It looked as if it had been cut up by an expert and not just by anyone hacking away.

Pres.: You talked about interference by the military authorities. Caliari states that Signori Marrata, Menotti Rigo and Tomellari were present when you talked about this.

Cacciatori: He's imagining things! I don't know either Rigo or Marrata.

Caliari: And Tomellari?

Cacciatori: He's my cousin. But I've never talked about such a thing. In any case, if I did, it would be a secret – and I would carry it to my grave.

Judge Ceccato: A secret?

Cacciatori: I never talked about that with Tomellari.

Caliari: It's Tomellari himself who said you did.

Cacciatori: Then he's telling wicked lies.

Sarfatti: There's no charge here by Cacciatori against Caliari. Might Cacciatori be saying that what Caliari said is a lie?

Cacciatori: No, I'm not. But I emphatically deny having said those things to anyone. I've retired to Peschiera with the intention of withdrawing from society and I don't want to come back to it at all.

It's evident that Cacciatori was trying to reconcile a loyalty to his convictions with a strong sense of 'duty' as a servant of the state. To do this he performed the most daring acrobatics: he denied that he had ever been pressured by the military authorities while at the same time he refused to call someone a liar – even when he had actually given evidence that they had lied.

He resigned and retired to Peschiera, to avoid being subjected to similar, endless acrobatics, trying simultaneously to salvage his 'honour' as a chief constable and his 'honour' as an honest man.

IX

In the meantime something new happened on 18 November. A certain Coronato Visco Gilardi approached a police officer called Carusi and told him that a few nights before the pieces of Isolina were retrieved from the Adige, he saw two men carrying a bag on the Lungadice Panvino.

But why come out with this now? Gilardi replied, 'I didn't think it was important. I let time pass. Meanwhile I thought about it. Then I thought it was all right to speak up, so I did. I spoke to Carusi and the examining magistrate.' 'And you took almost two years to make a decision!' the President pointed out. At that, Gilardi confessed that he had been frightened. 'Because of my work, I leave for home late at night – they would have given me the same treatment as Isolina.'

But briefly, what exactly did Gilardi see? Let us listen to his story. 'Towards 1.30 a.m. they closed the Café Smerzi where I work as a waiter. I accompanied my boss as far as his house in Vicolo Ponte Umberto I. Then I realized that I had forgotten the key to my house, which is in Via 20 Settembre. Well, since I had to begin work again at four, I decided to spend a sleepless night walking about. So I crossed Piazza Foggie, Corso Garibaldi, as far as Castelvecchio. The night was cold but clear, even though there was no moon. After I had gone a good bit along Lungadice Panvio and got near to the Garretta del Dazio, which overlooks the windmills of the Campagnola, I saw two figures in the distance, one tall and the other short. They were coming across Vicolo Ripa San Lorenzo towards the parapet of the city wall.

'At this point the wall is broken by a flight of steps leading down to the river and is flanked by an iron railing. I saw the smaller figure, who was carrying a bag, move forward. I thought it was probably something to do with smuggling; I was afraid and hid behind the sentry box, which had no soldier on guard that particular night. The two men looked around them and then, seeing that the wall where they were standing overlooked a conveniently wide flight of steps going down to the river, they went up to the railing on the steps and threw the bag over. I heard the plop as it hit the water. Then I heard one of them say "Now that's all done, we'll get the money".'

The next day *L'Adige* published two telegrams which said that 'a former mistress of Trivulzio's orderly states that the orderly confessed that he had thrown some bags in the Adige on orders from the lieutenant'.

In a special edition on 18 November *L'Adige* wrote: 'We are able to confirm the telegrams which arrived from Legnago. The lieutenant's orderly, Celeste Sitara, down from the mountains of San Bartolo dalla Montagna because he has been summoned by the defence and the public prosecutor, looks like becoming an important figure.'

But *L'Arena* had a strange method of proceeding. It also made this revelation with a great fanfare, but then rushed to pour water on the flames. It sent one of its journalists to Legnago to the Trattoria Due Mori where Favaretti worked (the former mistress of Sitara in whom he had confided about the bags). But then the journalist went after Sitara himself. And the next day he reported in *L'Arena* that Favaretti wouldn't have recognized the man even if he had gone right up to her and told her what a good-looking woman she was.

Favaretti was summoned by the judge and questioned. But she went back on everything she said, saying that she was only joking. What she really meant was that she was frightened.

Sitara was in fact someone to be frightened of. Small, robust, brutal, unscrupulous, he looked as though he would do anything for money.

Many of his friends in the barracks noticed that before Isolina's death, Sitara didn't have a penny and used to go begging cigar butts from his fellow soldiers. Cappelletti, an ordinary soldier, told the judges in his evidence that afterwards, Sitara 'had whole cigars to give away'.

But Sitara emphatically denied it. 'I have always been poor. Trivulzio used to give me 5 lire a month.'

What is more, a lot of soldiers knew that he spent whole nights away from the barracks even though this was not allowed. But this, too, Sitara emphatically denied. 'At most I might have been half an hour late when the lieutenant was on picket-duty.'

Sitara liked a drink. and when he got drunk, he became aggressive and sometimes loud. There were two witnesses, someone called Graziani, and the wife of the verger from Selva Progno, who said they heard him shouting at his sister who was asking him about the bags, 'Shut up, I don't know anything!' And when his mother insisted on knowing whether Trivulzio really had got Isolina pregnant, he smashed a glass shouting, 'I've told you before, I don't want to talk about it anymore!'

On another day, in an osteria in Badia Calavena, after he had had a few glasses of grappa, he let slip that he had thrown the bags from the Canossa courtyard on Trivulzio's orders. Emilio Corbellari, another soldier from the Alpini, was with him, and the next day Corbellari went and reported to the judge what he had said.

But what exactly did Sitara say to Corbellari? These are his words, which went on record. 'My master ordered me and another orderly to take the bags to the Adige. There were three masters, three lieutenants; at one point I felt something sticky on my hands and went up to a lamp and saw that the stuff was human flesh. Then as quickly as I could, I threw the bags into the Adige. After that I ran off to get paid by my master.'

Sarfatti and Caperle asked for Corbellari to be heard by the court. But they refused to call him, explaining that the trial was almost over and that it could not be reopened to call new witnesses.

In short, with regard to Sitara, two people, Coronato Gilardi and Cameri, manager of the Café Vittorio Emanuele, gave evidence in court that they saw two men carrying a bag which they then threw into the river on the night of the 14th.

Corbellari and Graziani gave evidence that they heard Sitara himself say that he had thrown the bags into the water on the orders of the 'three lieutenants'.

The last evidence concerning Sitara was that of Ettore Dalla Chiara, a court employee, who said that he was present at the first interrogation of the orderly during the preliminary investigation, and that he'd heard him say that he threw the bags in the Adige on behalf of 'my master'. This evidence of Dalla

Chiara's was confirmed by the owner of the Trattoria Alla Speranza and by the greengrocer Angelo Noventa, whom he told directly afterwards.

It would have been a simple matter to go and check the records. But as it has already been said, the records from the preliminary investigation were never brought into the court-room. And the lawyers defending Todeschini were never allowed to see them, no matter how many times they asked for them.

X

The witnesses in this trial sprang up like mushrooms. But they did not spontaneously appear in court. They were summoned and dragged in almost forcibly. They replied hesitatingly, reluc-tantly, revealing that they were afraid or bored. In fact, no one really wanted to be even remotely involved in this 'ugly busi-ness'.

The newspapers competed in making parallel inquiries and *L'Arena, Il Gazzettino* and *Verona del Popolo* all followed up various clues, which they kept from one another until the time was ripe to reveal them.

Nimini, for example, from *Verona del Popolo*, found a new witness named Carezzato, who said that on the night of the crime he saw five officers coming out of the Chiodo together. Moreover, he said that he ran into the owner of the Chiodo, Annibale Isotta, as he was cursing and saying 'Why did some-thing like this happen to me!'

The opposing side summoned the witness Burotto, a twenty-year-old sacristan from the Church of San Lorenzo who gave evidence that he heard Isolina say she was leaving home be-cause she was fed up with rows with her father.

But Burotto was so ingenuous that his evidence ended up rebounding on the people who summoned him. He calmly revealed that in fact he had been summoned to the lawyer

Trabucchi's office. It is worth hearing what he had to say.

Pres.: Do you remember anything else?
Burotto: No, I've already said it all to Lawyer Trabucchi.
Sarfatti: What do you mean, did Trabucchi send for you?
Burotto: Yes, with a letter brought from the Osteria Mutinelli.
Musatti: I request that this be put on record.
Sarfatti: Who questioned you?
Burotto: I saw four gentlemen round a table. I talked and they wrote it down, they made me sign it and I signed it just as I was told to do. (*Hilarity in the courtroom*)
Todeschini: Did they give you any money?
Burotto: Yes, 1 lira.
Todeschini: One lira for a quarter of an hour?
Burotto: Sir, they offered me a lira, and I said I don't want it. But they insisted and so I took it.
Sarfatti: How much do you earn per day?
Burotto: Sixty centèsimi.*
Sarfatti: Put it on record! And did you also complain that they gave Del Maggio 2 lire?
Burotto: Yes, sir. Then Lawyer Trabucchi said to me, If they ask you why I called you, tell them that you came here to visit the blind woman.

Trabucchi admitted to having paid witnesses but only 'for any inconvenience we caused them'.

Another witness called by Trivulzio's lawyers was the seamstress Vianello. She was aged 35 and had always worked at sewing underclothes. She said that she knew everything about Isolina because they lived in the same building.

Vianello launched into a crazy description of Isolina's lovers. 'The first evening I lived in that house I heard her bring in a lieutenant from the Bersaglieri and she kept him until two in the morning. Afterwards that particular lieutenant would often call on her. He would be with her until two or three in the morning. In 1899 she met Poli and they made such a racket in the house

*Sixty centèsimi = .60 lira

that we got very upset. Then a married lieutenant came to live
in the house and Isolina became very intimate with him. A
month later the officer left. She often went out and when she
got home she would say to Clelia, That captain of mine, my
captain, he's got me drunk, he's done this or that to me. There
was another officer who went on leave some time later. Isolina
and Poli then used the lieutenant's room and had four soldiers
from the Alpini in there. . . . One day she ordered an embroidered bodice from me! . . .'

Sarfatti: Did she have any particular requirements for this
bodice?
Vianello: These were her exact words: Make it large because I
hope I'm going to fill out and perhaps go and settle down in
Milan.
Pres.: What kind of a girl was Isolina?
Vianello: Flirtatious and loose. . . . She even blasphemed, she
had a habit of doing that.
Judge Ceccato: What impression did Trivulzio's arrest make on
you?
Vianello: I said immediately, They have made a mistake. If they
arrested him, they could have arrested all of them who had
anything to do with Isolina. Even during her relationship with
Lieutenant Trivulzio she carried on in her usual fashion. She
used to stand at her window, and she was always going out.

   Another witness, summoned by Trivulzio's lawyers, Matilde
Olivieri, was 23 years old and a waitress at the Trattoria Degli
Angeli. She was questioned on 17 November.

Pres.: Do you know Lieutenant Trivulzio?
Olivieri: I got to know him by chance once when I went out for
a walk with the lady I work for.
Pres.: Did he ever talk to you?
Olivieri: The lieutenant asked me in December 1899 if I would
like to make love with him. I said no because it seemed impossible to me that a lieutenant would have anything to do with a
serving woman.

Pres.: And then?

Olivieri: On the evening of January 16th (*the evening after Iso-lina's death*) he came to Corte Nogara and when he did not see me at the window, he rang the bell. I opened up but he did not come in. The bell rang a second time, I went down to close the door of the entrance hall and saw the lieutenant. I said hello to him and went out. At half past ten he rang a third time.

Pres.: He must have wanted to see you!

Pagani: Had he ever rung before?

Olivieri: No, never before. During the evening of the 17th he rang again. The second time I went down.

Judge Ceccato: Were you alone in the house then?

Olivieri: My mistress was also in.

Judge Ceccato: And what would have happened if she had gone down?

Olivieri: The lieutenant would have gone after her. . . . (*Hilarity in the courtroom*)

Pagani: Did the lieutenant go through the courtyard earlier?

Olivieri: He had been going back and forth for two months.

Pagani: And did he say a few words to you?

Olivieri: Yes.

Trivulzio: I rang the bell because she was not at the window as she usually was.

Olivieri: On the evening of the 18th I was going to get the newspaper as I do every evening, when the lieutenant came up to me and asked me if I would like to make love with him and I answered no again. Then I talked to him for an hour at my window.

Pres.: Did the lieutenant give you any money?

Olivieri: He gave me 20 lire when I was thrown out by my master and mistress after I was summoned as a witness.

Trivulzio: I had to mention Olivieri's name because the public prosecutor, who insisted on it, wanted to know where I spent my evenings.

Pagani: Did you, Olivieri, ever write to the lieutenant or ever commiserate with him in writing?

Olivieri: No, never. I don't know how to write and I never wrote to him.

Pagani: Here is a letter, Mr President, which Trivulzio received at the end of May 1900 and which is signed Matilde Olivieri. She asks for financial help in this letter.

Olivieri: I had money at that time, I was working. I didn't ask for money.

At this point, she was sent off. Some revelations, however, emerged from this questioning which throw light on Trivulzio's character: he wanted it known that on the same evening that Isolina's remains were found, he was making love to another woman, almost as if this were a sign of his innocence.

He got Olivieri thrown out of her job and gave her 20 lire in compensation. Then he put a letter from her into his lawyer's hands, in order to show that the girl was acting from self-interest, almost as if to suggest that she were 'selling herself'.

Just like Isolina, in fact. And he cut a figure as a generous, affable man who was always willing to help, a bit of a Don Juan, it's true, but that would be quite normal for a healthy young lieutenant like him.

The fact that his conquests were always poor and uneducated (Olivieri could not write, Isolina had had only a few years in school) did not mean that he was profiting from their situation, but his sense of chivalry took some testing with their continual demands for money. And to these he responded generously with gifts of 20, even 30 lire at a time.

XI

One of the mysteries of the Todeschini trial is the one concerning Emma Poli and her death. Her father maintained that as she was dying she revealed to him that she had been poisoned. And she gave two names: Ronconi and Zamboni. But the Zamboni who was picked out to appear in the trial obviously had nothing to do with it. And nothing more was known about

Ronconi. Neither was he called to testify. He was a doctor at the hospital where Poli died.

Benedetto Poli, who had been summoned to the trial, began by saying, 'First of all I want to protest against the rumour going around town that I've taken Trivulzio's side because I have been paid to do so.' This had a curiously hasty ring to it.

He attacked Felice Canuti, calling him a weak and useless father. He called Isolina 'that scorpion'. Lawyer Sarfatti reprimanded him, telling him to 'have some respect for the dead'.

But when he began to talk about Emma's death things got really murky.

Pres.: Where did your daughter Emma give birth?
Poli: They say Emma gave birth in Vicolo Sant'Angelo at her landlady Sabaini's house, but it was in Lungadice Porta Vittoria. It was the 22nd of January 1900, and later she died in hospital.
Pres.: Did you not go to see your daughter?
Poli: Yes, one day I went there and found her with a certain Magnanini and Doctor Ronconi – although the doctor taking care of her was Doctor Gozzi.
Judge Alfini: And what did Doctor Ronconi have to do with this?
Poli: He knows. . . . One day Doctor Gozzi said that Emma had to go into hospital to have an operation on her uterus. My daughter was amazed and said that she did not understand because four days previously she had got up – she could not understand how she could be in such a terrible state that she had to be taken into hospital.
Pres: So you went to the hospital to see her?
Poli: Yes, I went to the hospital. On the day I went there Emma said to me, I'm going to die, and if I die, Zamboni will be guilty. On the 17th or 18th of February, she kissed me and whispered in my ear, Papa, papa I'm dying, and I curse Zamboni and Ronconi.

At this point Poli came out with a fantastic story, told in a totally rambling fashion, about a meeting between Isolina, Emma, Zamboni and Ronconi. The men were supposed to have accused the two girls of infecting them with a venereal disease, and when they started to hit the girls Emma ran away, leaving Isolina in the hands of the two young men, one of whom was a doctor at the hospital where her friend later died.

The strange thing was that no one went more deeply into what Poli had recounted. No one asked to speak to Doctor Ronconi to clear up this story about the fight. Besides, it was the first time that another supposed lover of Isolina had been mentioned. Neither Clelia nor Policante ever brought him up. And neither, it must be said, did any of the neighbours, who were so busy spying out of windows and listening behind doors. Unless this was the famous medical lieutenant whose name no one ever managed to discover. . . . But everything is lost now in a maze of tangled facts.

Pres.: What happened after your daughter's death?
Poli: I forbade an autopsy on my dead daughter's body. I was afraid though that they might do it anyway. I went to the cemetery when it was time for the funeral and when they brought my daughter's coffin into the sacred ground I realized that Ronconi and Zamboni were there and I pointed them out to my brother-in-law as the ones who had ruined my daughter.

Something else is odd here: if Benedetto Poli knew Ronconi and Zamboni well enough to point them out to his brother-in-law, why then did he denounce another Zamboni who was much older, and what's more, a gentleman? But to return to the questioning.

Pres.: Did you go to the police station that day?
Poli: Yes. In the afternoon, I went to see Officers Bacchetti and Dallari, and asked them for information about what I had learned from my daughter on her deathbed. I also went to the public prosecutor. But without success.
Judge Ceccato: When did your daughter make these revelations?
Poli: Five or six days before her death.
Pres.: And why did you get angry with Zamboni?

Poli: I was convinced that when Emma mentioned Zamboni she meant either Cavalier Pietro, or his brother Luigi.
Pres.: Where do you believe Isolina's murder took place?

Here Benedetto Poli launched into a hurried, contradictory description which seemed tailored to draw suspicion away from the Chiodo and Trivulzio.

Poli: From my investigations, I am convinced that the crime happened in Vicolo Sant'Andrea. In fact my daughter thought that the customers who used to go to the Osteria Sabaini, and whom she had often seen talking to Zamboni and Ronconi, were all responsible. When they closed the osteria I went to look over the ground floor of the place and found a little room which had been papered over. They did not want to show me the wine shop. Then the examining magistrate showed me a letter from Emma in which she invited Isolina to Vicolo Sant' Andrea. They also found another letter at the Canutis' house from Doctor Ronconi, inviting Isolina somewhere, but we don't know where.
Pres.: From whom did you learn this?
Poli: From Trivulzio, when I was friendly with his defence lawyer Tassistro.

So it was true, as he said at the beginning of the interrogation, that he had had talks with Trivulzio's defence lawyers. Whether he was paid or not, he did repeat their arguments and their version of the facts in the courtroom: that the murder did not happen at the Chiodo but rather in another trattoria. (It's not understood why the Osteria Sabaini was picked, whether for some precise reason or at random in order to create confusion.)

Naturally the lawyers on the other side asked to see the letters to which Trivulzio and Poli referred. But the letters did not turn up. They asked to see Emma Poli's post-mortem examination chart. But this did not turn up either, at this point or later.

Poli, with his contradictions, his lies, his muddles, was allowed to go. We shall never know up to what point he told the truth. The only thing that he repeated right from the beginning was what his daughter had told him, that she had been poisoned in hospital. But everything else that followed was too confused to give a clear picture of how things happened. As for the doctors Ronconi and Zamboni, here the knot becomes even more impossible to untangle. And the only ones who could have denied or confirmed what Poli said – Ronconi and the young Zamboni who was at the hospital when Poli was there – were never summoned to give evidence.

XII

The last witness was the landlord Francesco Gobbi from Ronco d'Adige. His evidence is extremely important. It concerns the place where the crime was committed, the Chiodo Restaurant, and its owner Annibale Isotta.

Gobbi said that he had heard about a room for officers that was closed to the public and decided to go and see it. 'So I went for lunch at the Chiodo. I sat down in this little room and Isotta came at once and sat down next to me. I asked him about the room. First he talked about wine. Then, when I saw that he was a bit depressed I asked him, "And how are things going here?" "Ah," he said, "my wife's ill and things aren't too good." "Is this the place where they cut up Isolina?" "It's the room where Isolina and another girl and three gentlemen were having a good time, dancing and doing who knows what." "What happened?" I asked. "They stripped her naked, then they took a fork and stuck it inside her and . . ." I asked to see the room. As he crossed in front of me, he pointed out the door and said, "They carried her through this door out into the street." I paid my bill and left.'

They summoned Isotta, and the two landlords were made to confront each other. Both were fat, with round faces, just as you would expect in a landlord.

Pres.: Gobbi, do you confirm what you said now that you're face to face with Isotta?

Gobbi: It's as I said, I'm afraid.

Isotta: It's all lies.

Gobbi: After he denied it three times before the examining magistrate, Isotta agreed that he had told me that the whole world including Verona said the business occurred at the Chiodo.

Isotta admitted to having complained about rumours which were going around about his restaurant. But nothing else.

Gobbi insisted that not only did Isotto tell him what he reported in court, but that he also threatened him on the stairs: if he talked he would 'cop it'. 'Then Dallari, who was sent by the court, came to my house to tell me that I should be a little careful as regards Isotta and his restaurant.'

The police officer Dallari was then called. The president asked him if he had talked to Gobbi. Dallari said yes. 'And what did you say to him?' 'That he should have some respect for Isotta because he's the person who has been damaged the most by the whole business.'

He was then asked if he knew that Isotta threatened Gobbi. 'I understood that in the office at the police station Isotta said 'That murderer Gobbi has ruined me.' 'And did you repeat this to Gobbi?' 'I might have, I don't remember.'

As Gobbi said that his wife Virginia was present while it happened, Signora Virginia Gobbi was called. The woman confirmed what her husband had said.

Gobbi quoted another witness, Count Polfranceschi, to whom he spoke when he returned from the Chiodo. Count Polfranceschi was called. He said that it was true, he had heard Gobbi's story, just as he told it to the judges, the day after the two landlords had met. To a question put by Judge Ceccato on what he thought about Gobbi as a person, the Count replied 'He is an extremely sane, frank and sincere person.'

Gaetano Rossi from Ronco d'Adige also confirmed that he had heard Gobbi's story, 'which made a deep impression on him' a few hours after he had come back from the Chiodo. And to the question 'What opinion do you have of Gobbi?' he replied, 'I consider him to be an honest and sincere man.'

An expert who had visited the Chiodo just after Isolina's murder was called to give evidence. This man, Pedrotti, said yes, there was a room under the stairs in the restaurant, with a door which led from the little room between the officers' room and that of the Chiodo Society. 'From the little room under the stairs you could go down into the cellar and also leave by another door leading into the hall of the house next door in Vicolo Chiodo.'

The president turned to landlord Isotta. 'You never mentioned this little room under the stairs.' And Isotta replied, 'I never mentioned it because the door was always kept shut. For me it was as if it did not exist.' The president: 'Do you realize that this is a serious omission?' 'I didn't think it was important,' replied Isotta, mortified.

XIII

On 12 December the lawyers began their summing up. First it was the turn of Trabucchi, Trivulzio's lawyer. His defence of the lieutenant had a secure foundation on the evidence given by Doctor Bonuzzi, who maintained that Isolina's pregnancy was of six, perhaps seven months' duration when she died.

This expert opinion was contradicted by other specialists. But Trabucchi seemed to consider it superior to all those offered by the doctors called to give evidence.

There was also the fact that Bonuzzi had always appeared willing to help Trivulzio's lawyers in any way. He maintained in court that Carlini, one of the witnesses on Isolina's side, was of a 'neurotic disposition' and was therefore unreliable. He was unforthcoming, practically mute, on what he knew about Emma Poli's death. He could only manage to say that it was a case of 'puerperal fever'.

A lawyer pointed out to him that the girl's father had said his daughter had been better for four days and had got up. 'Do you know anything about why she was taken into hospital for an operation on her uterus, as Doctor Gozzi told Poli?'

Bonuzzi replied that he knew nothing. He knew only that the girl died from puerperal fever. So where were her case notes? he was asked. No reply. They must have been lost. But if it had been a case of puerperal fever, why had Doctor Gozzi talked about an operation on her uterus? No reply.

Trabucchi used Bonuzzi's second statement to maintain that Trivulzio could not be the father of the child. 'Given that Trivulzio only went to live in the Canutis' house towards the middle of September, and Isolina died when she was six months pregnant, that means she was pregnant before knowing Trivulzio.' To give greater credibility to his theory, he called as a witness the laundryman Zampieri who washed the clothes belonging to the Canuti household.

Lorenzo Zampieri was 32 years old with a wife and two children. He stated that since he had not seen any blood-stained cloths belonging to Isolina in September, he came to the conclusion that she had been pregnant from the beginning of the month.

Paroli: You are the laundryman for the Canuti household?
Zampieri: That's right. After that last week in August or the first week in September I didn't see any more of that particular stained linen.
P.M.: Who used to give you the washing?
Zampieri: Sometimes it was Isolina, sometimes Clelia, because Isolina would say, You go so that I can stand here on the balcony and watch out for my lovers.
Musatti: How many families bring you their laundry, Zampieri?
Zampieri: Sixty or seventy.
Musatti: And how many people work for you?
Zampieri: Myself, my wife, my daughter, and another woman. At one time my daughter used to go to the Canutis' house, but then I made her stop because Isolina was causing a scandal. She also spread wicked rumours about me. (*The room rocked with laughter.*)

Pagani: What sort of things did she say?

Zampieri: She would say, Laundryman, my sweetheart has left me. And I replied, But you've got a new one every day, so why worry? One day she would talk to me about the Bersaglieri, the next about the Alpini. I advised her not to say anything to her father because he would beat her. I tried to give her good advice, but then I stopped because it was wasting time that I should have been spending working.

Todeschini: And you keep a check on the washing of sixty families?

Zampieri: Well, I know them all.

Todeschini: And you are quite sure that Isolina stopped having her period in September? You don't have a single doubt, not a trace of uncertainty, despite looking after so many families?

Zampieri: I'm sure.

Todeschini: In that case, you were spying on her.

Zampieri: No. But I noticed that at the end of August Isolina's cloths were clean.

Todeschini: May I mention someone who approached you before you gave evidence? Could it be Lawyer Trabucchi, by any chance, who has a nice habit of making payments to witnesses? Did he give you anything?

Zampieri: I don't know anything about lawyers. I'm telling you what I know.

For the rest of the time Trabucchi pressed on very confidently. Policante was a 'witch', a real 'devil in skirts'. 'I am convinced', said Trabucchi, 'that Maria Policante may have given her victim, Isolina, the idea of pinning the blame on to Lieutenant Trivulzio by trying to deflect responsibility from herself by means of her various statements.'

But the surprise came at the end. Maria Policante could not be a credible witness because many years ago she was convicted of theft and of 'insulting sentries'.

Musatti intervened to explain that she stole a branch from a tree when she was eighteen. And in addition, that the insult was a sharp retort to a guard who had come up to her to make her an obscene suggestion. But Trabucchi paid no attention to

Musatti. According to him, 'You can't believe a criminal, gentlemen of the court, because naturally she does not tell the truth.'

As for Clelia's statements, which were extremely important, he dismissed them by saying that 'this is reported speech . . . she could easily have misheard; in short, there is nothing definite in her evidence'.

The revelations made by the landlord Gobbi about Isotta were 'fantasy'. Besides, Isotta had denied everything, therefore it was not true. Sitara could not have said things that he had an interest in keeping quiet. Therefore, the witnesses they heard are liars. The person who saw the figures with the bags 'must have been dreaming'. Especially the one who saw Sitara go into the Canossa Palace. In fact, the palace night-watchman maintained in court that the gate was closed every night at eight o'clock. Therefore anyone who claimed the contrary was either 'drunk or telling lies'.

XIV

On 13 December it was Lawyer Tassistro's turn. He launched into a speech which was emphatically sentimental. It began: 'Trivulzio has already been punished enough for a crime he did not commit. We shall now begin to rebuild his reputation and shall not allow his enemies to remain in hiding. This was said by an old woman as she clasped Trivulzio's hands . . . his old mother. And this is our wish too, for judgment to fall unmercifully on those who were without mercy. . . .'

As far as Lawyer Tassistro was concerned, the real culprit in the whole business was Policante. 'Just imagine before you the figures of Carlo Trivulzio and Policante before January 14th, and ask whether you are prepared to accept what the woman says as reliable and truthful. The word of an officer should carry more weight than the oath of a Policante. . . .'

As for the Chiodo, 'We have two contradictory statements, that of one landlord against another. It does not hold water.'

On 17 December Lawyer Pagani-Cesa continued his summing up. 'The trial has shown that Trivulzio had absolutely no reason to be concerned about Isolina's condition, given the notorious life she led, and the numbers of lovers she had.'

For Pagani, the whole trial was a political affair, 'a manoeuvre on the part of the socialists to discredit the army'. He talked about a 'socialist police force' composed of journalists and time-wasters who had 'the nerve to stand in for the State's police force'. They had been forestalled because they believed in Trivulzio's guilt, while all the witnesses they had discovered were shown to have little credibility.

'As far as we are concerned, Trivulzio acted correctly in regard to the death, reacted calmly to the news of her death, showed the same calm confidence to those who unjustly handcuffed him, and finally deservedly celebrated his freedom when he regained it . . . to us all this seems like the conduct of an innocent person. It simply remains for me to make a comparison between this proud, dignified behaviour and that of his heartless enemies. . . . Look how Trivulzio also solemnly swore his innocence to Lieutenant Marchiosi on the head of his old mother when he was in camp high up in the mountains. . . .'

Isolina was a girl 'with few morals' who attributed her pregnancy to the lieutenant solely in order to 'tap him for money'.

As for Sitara, the lawyers on the opposing side wanted to speculate about the fact that his financial situation had changed. But this change consisted only in the fact that 'earlier Sitara smoked butts and later, whole cigars'. But that should have come as no surprise to anyone, because a small amount of money had been given to him by 'his mamma' who had saved up the lire to make him a present.

Carlini was a 'pathologically neurotic case' and therefore untrustworthy. 'Professor Bonuzzi reiterates this, adding that we are dealing with a weak and therefore suggestible personality. On this point I would like to quote the opinion of the famous clinician, Professor Ottolenghi, who talks about the particular suggestibility of pathologically neurotic cases who are convinced that they see things which, in reality, they do not see. So I say, it is not that Carlini gives evidence that is not true, but can

Carlini be fully believed? Is he not a pathologically neurotic case?'

The words 'pathologically neurotic case' appealed to the lawyer Pagani-Cesa very much and he used them against anyone whose evidence could be damaging to Trivulzio. Even the crowd which filled the courtroom was 'pathologically neurotic'. 'During this private investigation lasting ten months, Trivulzio's enemies have been helped by the mass. The crowd is subject to a pathological phenomenon: it is carried away by suggestions, which surround and completely invade it. It is always an instrument in the hands of passionate and suggestible people. . . .'

XV

It was now the turn of the defence to speak. The first to begin was Lawyer Caperle, who asked 'But who was Isolina?', and continued: 'A girl deprived of a mother's tenderness, with a father who was always absent at work . . . Isolina was a warmhearted girl who liked dancing and flirtations. But nothing more.'

On the other hand, who was Trivulzio? 'A lieutenant in the Alpini regiment who was much loved by his comrades. But we cannot be less than somewhat surprised at his behaviour towards Isolina. Trivulzio knows that his girlfriend has disappeared, he knows that the remains found in the Adige might be those of poor Isolina, and he feels neither pity nor pain for the girl he had held in his arms, but goes and has a good time and, on the evening of his arrest, goes to amuse himself at Cavalchina. . . .'

It is obvious that Todeschini's lawyers were also prone to rhetoric and sentimentality. They felt the need, as if the evidence and the facts were not enough, to tug at the public's heart-strings in the already overheated atmosphere of the courtroom.

The tone changed dramatically with the arrival of Lawyer Sarfatti who was the most cautious and rational of the lawyers opposing Trivulzio. Sarfatti neither made statements about principles, nor tried to appeal to the public's feelings, but went back to the facts, to the evidence, with a meticulousness that was almost pernickety.

'Trivulzio's alibi rests on his demonstrating that during that period he was at various places where he could not have committed the crime. But have you shown how the lieutenant spent the other hours of the crime? The witness Mutinelli kept an eye on the lieutenant's comings and goings and he made these clear. But could he say what Trivulzio might have done during the hours he was out? It is not up to us to do this, it is for you to establish where Trivulzio was minute by minute, and you have not done that. . . .'

As for the Chiodo, the witness Carezzato saw Trivulzio leave it with four officers on the evening of the 14th. 'The evening of the 14th he was on picket-duty, but it cannot be said that an officer on picket-duty is unable to leave his post. Anyway if Trivulzio was on picket-duty that evening, his orderly, Sitara was not.'

Clelia Canuti's evidence revealed that Trivulzio 'began to have sexual relations with Isolina three or four days after he came to the Canutis' house and maintained them up to the eve of her disappearance. . . . Two years after that horrible misfortune it is possible that poor Clelia might forget a few things, or not be quite as precise, but her testimony is basically unassailable.' In fact no one ever did take issue with it.

It was Clelia who said that Isolina confided in her that on two occasions Trivulzio gave her money, once 10 lire, and another time 25 in order to buy the powder to induce an abortion.

It was Clelia who reported what Trivulzio said to Isolina, 'If you won't have an abortion here in Verona you can go to Milan where the women do a good job of it.' And Clelia saw the powder. Trivulzio also saw it. Not only that, but the lieutenant also admitted during questioning that he had talked about Verona and Milan. He himself says that he would have advised a 'change of air'. He only denied the motivation for this change of air. 'It seems to us that this makes everything perfectly clear.'

As for Nimini, whom the lawyers on the opposing side tried to discredit in every possible way because he was obviously unafraid, he said that he saw five officers come out of the Chiodo Restaurant on the evening of the 15th. And one of them was Trivulzio.

'We have the testimony of the landlord Gobbi who relates how Isotta confided in him about the orgy at the Chiodo, about the attempted abortion with the fork and about the girl's death.

'The gravity of what Gobbi said is demonstrated by the fact that Isotta denied even knowing him three times before the examining magistrate. Then he admitted it.

'You brought in waiters from the Chiodo as witnesses to show that Gobbi was not telling the truth. But what is the evidence of the waiters and the cook worth, when they like Isotta and have been dependent on him for so many years?' Besides, they would risk their jobs, either because they would be sacked by an angry employer or because the restaurant might be closed down by the police.

One of the waiters said in front of two witnesses, Leoni Giuseppe and Perugini Luigi, that he had seen Isolina with Trivulzio at the Chiodo. But 'at the hearing he thought it better to deny what would go down on record'.

Then there was the witness Cameri who saw three people carrying bags cross the Cavour courtyard and go into the Canossa Palace. The public prosecutor brought in the evidence of the night-watchman who maintained that the gate was regularly closed at night. 'But there is nothing to stop a caretaker from forgetting. And then we have other witnesses here who before your very eyes declare that they saw the gate open that night.

'But whether or not the hypothesis concerning the Chiodo is true, we maintain that Lieutenant Trivulzio was involved in an attempted abortion, which inescapably led to Isolina's death. We maintain that he must know this and that there is no element of slander in our assertion.'

XVI

Next Musatti tried to examine more closely the facts concerning Isolina's 'morality', in view of the atmosphere of disapproval towards the murdered girl, which was almost palpable in the courtroom.

'They wanted to prove that when they were living in the Via Disciplina Isolina and Policante caused a scandal with their behaviour. But we could also say that it's extremely easy, in summer-time, to surprise someone at their window in their shirt-sleeves or even naked. . . .

'The witness Sterzi saw Trivulzio and Isolina together from his window. And he says that he saw Trivulzio retreat, nauseated. Now I ask you, how could a witness see Trivulzio's nausea from another window?'

As he continued to analyse the facts, it was obvious that Isolina was not at all the prostitute that people would believe, but rather a romantic girl who easily fell in love. And in any case, only two lovers came to light: the lieutenant from the Bersaglieri regiment, Petrini, who was the first and then left for Ancona, and Lieutenant Trivulzio, by whom she became pregnant and whom she hoped to marry so that she could keep the baby.

'As for the medical lieutenant whose name we never succeeded in verifying, whose shadow somehow escapes us in a sinister fashion (let's remember here that all the experts said the dissection of the body was carried out by a skilled hand, by a surgeon), he certainly courted Isolina but he only had one kiss, which he got by blackmailing her.'

The most serious witness for the prosecution, however, was Trivulzio's own orderly, Celeste Sitara. 'He contradicted himself on more than one occasion in the most stupid fashion, whether it was about the bags or his going out at night. We learn that more than once, after he had been drinking, he talked about the bags and the orders he had received from the three officers. There are more than five people who have come here to give evidence about his confession. It seems to us that this is enough at least to throw doubt upon the lieutenant's veracity.'

But let's get on to Trivulzio and his behaviour at the Canutis' house. 'He displays indifference, coldness and condescension.' He made love to Isolina but without committing himself, even despising her. He called her 'little scorpion, monkey'. When the remains were discovered he showed absolute indifference and was completely lacking in feeling about it. Everyone but he was upset by it, and he was the one who had held her in his arms right up to the previous day. He sent Sitara to make enquiries. But Sitara went to Isolina's father and, rather than making enquiries, he told him that it was nothing to do with her, so the enquiries ended.

'When he was arrested Trivulzio showed above all coldness and self-control. His fellow officers put this forward as proof of his innocence. But it seems to me that indifference and coldness might well hide other weaknesses. He laughs impudently in this courtroom, appears self-confident, never penitent, never sorry, never moved. His manner is cold and derisive. This does not seem to me to be the behaviour of someone who is innocent, but rather someone who is defying the entire world, and knows he is getting away with it.

'When he's released he goes to the Chiodo where he sings their triumphal song and drinks toasts to his freedom.

'Trivulzio, they say, has tried to rehabilitate himself. But how? With the memorandum to the Minister? We have never seen it. In his association with the public prosecutor in the Zamboni business? With the proceedings against *Verona del Popolo*? But he only undertook these when his position had become untenable. For months Todeschini provoked him in order to get him to start proceedings. And only after two years did he start proceedings, when not to do so would have been an admission of guilt.

'Trivulzio has tried to throw all the blame on to Maria Policante. And his lawyers have tried to confirm this. But let's look at the facts. We know that on the 7th, Policante went to the Canutis' house to ask for news about Isolina. And we know that she went back on the following days and advised old Canuti to go and speak to the lieutenant who was Isolina's "sweetheart".

'If she had been guilty, some piece of evidence would have

emerged against her. While all that can be held against her, finally, is that she once showed herself naked at her window, had some lovers who were soldiers, as do nearly all the women servants in our city, bought some sweet mustard for her friend Isolina, had an abortion at the hands of the midwife Friedman, and swore at a policeman when he bothered her.'

Finally, even Musatti put forward that he did not consider Trivulzio to be guilty of murder but that he definitely thought he was implicated in Isolina's abortion. 'There are too many clues which shout this out. And what *Verona del Popolo* clearly spelled out, other newspapers also wrote about. The lieutenant's position in this affair is very questionable. Therefore we believe that no malice exists on Todeschini's part in his description of the facts.'

XVII

When it was the prosecution's turn again, the lawyers had no idea what line to take, and so they came up with some extremely risky hypotheses. For example, Paroli based his summing up on the hypothesis that Isolina was not in fact dead and therefore Trivulzio was innocent.

'Has it been legally proved that Isolina's dead?' he shouted at a disconcerted public. 'Cavalier Cacciatori says that no one disappeared at that time, but we cannot know this with certainty. How many girls disappear and are not reported!

'Second point: they found a curvature of the spine in the remains, and Isolina had such a curvature. But doesn't a body change during pregnancy? There is nothing more normal than a pregnant woman undergoing a change like this because of the weight of the pregnancy.

'Third point: the shopping list. Do you really think that the perpetrators of such a crime would be so naïve as to leave a list in the victim's handwriting on the body after it had been cut up into pieces? It's obvious that the list was put there expressly to divert attention and to make people believe that this was Isolina's body.

'Even the clothes could have been made into a bundle to make one think that this was Isolina Canuti.'

But what would be the purpose of such convoluted behaviour? he was asked. He replied quickly: to implicate Trivulzio, to make him guilty when he was innocent, to create artificially 'a murderer out of a most noble and courageous servant of our army'.

As for the witnesses, Paroli continued, it was clear that they were either all ill or alcoholic or mad. Clelia was obviously a girl who was a bit 'simple-minded', and it was not possible to believe what she said. Gobbi 'had definitely drunk a bit too much of that good wine which he keeps in his cellar'. He was the only one to have talked about an orgy at the Chiodo. The business with the fork was his own invention, 'an absolutely fantastic and incredible idea'. On the other hand, Annibale Isotta, the owner of the Chiodo, who was a discreet, responsible person, denied what Gobbi said more than once, and so did his waiters and his cook.

As for Sitara, it was evident that he was a sensible orderly who was sure of himself, who would never, on his own initiative, have said the things they wanted to attribute to him. Besides, he denied everything. Those who saw him that night could only have been hallucinating, or drunk, if not also lying.

'In fact, you have destroyed yourselves, because your evidence has shown you to be empty-handed, and so you have had to resort to your Madonna to save you, and her name is Maria Policante!' (*Applause in the courtroom*)

The atmosphere in the room had in fact changed. At the beginning of the trial the public was all on Isolina's side, against Trivulzio. Now, more and more it was influenced by what the lawyers for the prosecution had to say.

Musatti accused the courtroom attendants of controlling the tickets. He claimed that there was a kind of selection going on which allowed in those who were on Trivulzio's side and kept the others outside.

The fact is that over those last few days the lawyers who were defending Todeschini were listened to reluctantly. The stentorian voice of Trabucchi on the other hand, inspired neverending applause.

Trabucchi attacked Todeschini head on, accusing him of being an anti-militarist. 'Our honourable friend has already been sentenced to three years' imprisonment for failing to report for the draft and for anti-militarist propaganda. Furthermore, anti-militarism is one of the creeds of his socialist newspaper.'

So it is very clear that all Todeschini's enquiries were not aimed at finding out the truth about Isolina, but were seeking to discredit Trivulzio, and with him, the army.

Trivulzio is innocent, Trabucchi continued, because Isolina had many lovers and the baby was certainly not his. We have had proof of her loose morals in this very courtroom from various witnesses. The seamstress Vianello, Di Maggio and the fruiterer Elisa Cacciatori – all have said that Isolina had many lovers. Lucia Saletti, another neighbour, testified that Trivulzio's arrest came like a bolt from the blue because everyone in the neighbourhood knew that Isolina had a huge number of lovers. Another neighbour said that all the soldiers in the Bersaglieri regiment knew Isolina and spoke to her in a familiar manner.

'Trivulzio, who was completely innocent, found himself in this ugly situation! One day when he was ordered to stay at home and was reading D'Annunzio on his bed, Isolina came and offered herself to him and he succumbed. And he's to be blamed for this!

'Yes, they tried to portray Trivulzio as a cynic, a bloodthirsty man who said, according to Policante, that you could buy anything with money, even a man's death. But do you believe that if Trivulzio had promised thousands of lire, he would be reduced to giving away the famous 10 lire to Policante in order to save her sewing machine from being taken by the bailiffs . . .?

'I do not know what happened, no one knows, but if you think about Policante's intimacy with the midwife Friedman, and if you remember that the midwife's son is someone who dissects bodies, you might come to the conclusion that Isolina could have been involved in an attempted abortion. But it is certainly improbable that she went to get an abortion without confiding in Policante, who was her best friend and who certainly knows the real author of this foul crime.' (*Frenzied applause*)

XVIII

By some mysterious alchemy, the public filling the hall once more reversed its position in the last few days, to side with Todeschini unreservedly.

Sarfatti began to speak again. 'The accused wanted to portray Isolina as someone who was greedy for money, and for us to see Policante as a procuress. But what can you say about those captains and lieutenants who would enjoy a woman right under little Clelia's nose? Those officers, Petrini and Trivulzio, rent a room at the Canutis' house and take Isolina along with the furniture, Isolina, whose funeral oration was "little cow".'

The public applauded wildly. The lawyer continued: 'It has been clearly shown that Isolina did not want to have an abortion. If she did go looking for a woman to carry out an abortion, it was because she was obeying something stronger than herself, and that something was Lieutenant Trivulzio's will. But meanwhile, the fact remains that you have never brought a legal action against Policante who, as far as you are concerned, is an awkward witness. And in addition, you actually used her evidence when it was convenient, even though you destroyed her credibility as a witness.'

More applause accompanied this speech. A voice was heard shouting from the huddle of lawyers. 'You're a windbag. You've always been a windbag and you always will be!'

It was Lawyer Pagani's voice.

Sarfatti replied swiftly, 'And you'll always have the wind taken out of your sails!' which raised a storm of laughter and applause.

'If Policante were your enemy, she would not have denied
that Trivulzio gave her a job to do,' Sarfatti continued, after an
interruption which highlighted the macho spirit of rivalry between the lawyers.

'Maria Policante goes to De Mori's and asks her to perform an
abortion for a young woman, the "sweetheart" of a lieutenant.
And it is only two days later that Policante gives her Trivulzio's
name, because the midwife insists on knowing. And De Mori
herself confirmed this in this courtroom. If Policante had
wanted to build up false evidence against the lieutenant, she
would have come out with his name immediately and not
waited to be asked so insistently for it.

'As for Isolina's morality, the fact remains that we know
about only two people who slept with her. The rest is gossip.
No one but Trivulzio could be responsible for the pregnancy.
Besides, he himself has never denied either the business with
the powder, or his advising her to go to Milan. In addition, he
said in court that he saw in that notebook, Isolina's diary, the
date when she first missed her period: the first of November. . . . And furthermore, we have Isolina, who was so much
in love with the lieutenant that she prepared zabaglione for him
with marsala and eggs her father had bought for the other
children.'

At this, Trivulzio jumped to his feet shouting.

Trivulzio: Not at their expense, at mine if anything!
Sarfatti: Don't interrupt, and don't be so arrogant!
Trivulzio: Then leave the zabaglione out of it. I never had any of it!
Sarfatti: I'll say what suits me even if you'd like it kept quiet!
Trivulzio: Neither I nor my friends have ever accepted any-
thing from the Canutis!
Sarfatti: Listen to this brotherly love pouring forth! That's
enough!

The public whistled and booed the lieutenant. The president
threatened to empty the hall and continue behind closed doors.
But then he reconsidered and went back to his seat and the
public remained in the courtroom.

Sarfatti continued to show that Isolina was obviously taken with Trivulzio, that she did not want to have an abortion, and that even if there had been a medical lieutenant courting her, she really did keep her distance from him because she was in love with Trivulzio.

But here Trivulzio interrupted again, shouting energetically from his seat, 'But everybody had her. It's been proved, it's been proved!'

P.M.: Stop that Lieutenant Trivulzio, it's disgraceful!

The public interrupted with more whistling. The lawyers hurled insults at one another. There was a fight in the air. The atmosphere became white-hot. It was now almost time for the sentence and everyone was tense: the public, the judges, the lawyers. After cohabiting for almost two months, both weariness and intolerance had settled in.

It seemed that Sarfatti was now reiterating facts known only too well, even if his sharp intelligence did focus in detail on finding arguments the others had not emphasized.

'In addition, I wonder how it was that Trivulzio never talked to his military comrades about Isolina's disappearance? Were the army, which was like a family to him, and the captain, who was like a father, perhaps unworthy of his confidences? He would tell his friends everything but felt it unnecessary to let them know that his mistress had disappeared. . . . If that's not enough, I'd like you to take into consideration the lieutenant's attitude during the trial: arrogant, cold, cutting, aggressive. He has never shown the least sympathy and pity for poor Isolina – who was actually his mistress for months – not by a single gesture of sorrow or humility.'

Sarfatti's place was taken by Borciani who was to make the last summing up for the public prosecutor. Borciani highlighted the fact that if *Verona del Popolo* was accused of having provoked Lieutenant Trivulzio, it did nothing other than report things that were already reported in other newspapers, starting with *L'Arena*, which nowadays was so zealous in defending the rights of the Alpini regiment.

On 22 October even *L'Adige* hurled itself into the fray against those who wanted to see the case buried. So did the *Corriere della Sera* and *Resto del Carlino*. All the pieces of evidence that weighed so heavily against Trivulzio were reproduced in these newspapers. Even *L'Arena* talked about 'extraordinary revelations' concerning the orderly Sitara on 27 January.

'Seen objectively, the evidence against Trivulzio was serious, and this evidence is unchanged a year later. . . . If one day a novelist were to write about what happened, he might entitle his first chapter: 'The wall which spoke'. Trivulzio's name was in fact written on the wall by De Mori, and the midwife has never denied this. The name was seen by someone from the police called Dallari and this alone would be enough to implicate him in Isolina's abortion.

'And what can we say about Clelia Canuti? He has never taken proceedings against her nor accused her of telling lies. But she actually said here in the courtroom that she heard Trivulzio talk about a powder to bring on an abortion, "and if it doesn't work, you'll go to Milan". What would Clelia stand to gain by lying? And why would Isolina go crying to her, telling her that Trivulzio wanted her to have an abortion and that she had dreamed of a happiness which perhaps she hadn't dared hope for? What interest did she have in lying? Policante also repeated to you what Clelia said.

'But the most important witness against you is Trivulzio himself, for the simple reason that he has admitted everything, denying only his direct participation in events that he could not possibly declare false. He did not deny that he talked about abortion to Isolina; he did not deny that he talked about the powder; he did not deny that he advised her to "have a change of air"; he did not even deny that he comforted her father by saying to him, "Don't worry, Isolina's somewhere safe"; and finally, he did not even deny that he gave her money – the 25 lire that Isolina used to buy the powder.

'All this is incriminating evidence, showing that Trivulzio procured an abortion. And if you then tell me that he's an honest person and not a criminal I shall tell you that abortion is considered a trifle by a certain class of people. He himself said:

"It's like spitting on the ground. . . ." However, I wonder if it's so impossible to believe that an officer who is the soul of politeness with the ladies and who gets involved with women servants in exchange for money, could possibly be a scoundrel. . . . Trivulzio could easily reply truthfully to various accusations: I wasn't thinking straight when I helped with the abortion and didn't advise against it, but I don't know anything about anything else. But the fact that he denies even this is so suspicious that it makes him a suspect for the second crime too. . . .

'And how can we overlook the fact that on the very day that Isolina's remains were discovered the lieutenant hurried off to find Mathilde Olivieri and asked her for love and kisses as if they were absolutely essential to him? And he continued in the same fashion on the evenings that followed. . . . Do you know why the State Prosecutor glossed over this business? Because Olivieri testified something that is extremely damaging to Trivulzio. He was looking for an alibi; he wanted another lover to present to the examining magistrate. Is this man's behaviour not obviously suspicious . . .? He remains impassive, pipe in mouth, when he hears the news about the body being discovered and says, "I know nothing." This proves that he was lying. Anyone else in his place would have had some reaction, even and especially if he were innocent. . . . So we come to January 21st, when rumours of the new version of the facts were already circulating. Trivulzio could not ignore these rumours. *L'Arena* then printed an obvious piece of information about Isolina Canuti. Trivulzio must have been, however innocent, afraid of being implicated in this business, and could not possibly be cheerful, carefree or indifferent.

'The lieutenant goes to prison, comes out, and his behaviour is always coldly self-confident. He knows how to keep up the pretence very well. He thinks that the thing is to keep quiet. He is counting on silence and oblivion. But there is someone who does not want to keep quiet. One newspaper pursues him with more or less explicit provocation. *Verona del Popolo* asks that the trial be re-opened in order to shed some light on this horrible business. He continues to remain silent. For months he keeps quiet. Until finally, his position becomes so difficult that he has to take a stand. The lawsuit against the newspaper begins. But not against the people who make the biggest accusations against him, Policante and Clelia Canuti. Only later does he make up his mind to bring an action against Policante, but the trial is an almighty fiasco because the authorities undertaking the inquiry do not consider the accusation against the woman to be a valid one.

'In short, it seems to us that we have shown that Mario Todeschini wanted to clarify events with his articles and to find the truth, not to libel Trivulzio. We ask for justice and a fair judgment!'

The end of Borciani's summing up was received with applause. Shouting 'Hurray!' the crowd accompanied him to his hotel.

On 20 December came Lawyer Paroli's reply. He went back to defending the absolute innocence of Trivulzio and presenting Policante as a fiend. The crowd interrupted him with shouts of 'That's enough, that's enough, you buffoon!' But he carried on regardless. The public continued to be noisy. The president threatened to empty the courtroom. Pagani said loudly, having turned to face the crowd, 'It's only natural that the public doesn't understand!' There was another outburst of boos and whistling.

When Lawyer Paroli stopped talking it was almost seven o'clock and the hall had emptied. 'I know that I do not have the crowd's approval' were his last words before ending, 'but I shall never lower myself to obtain it. As I steadfastly turn my face towards Justice I feel some bitterness, but she is the only woman in this trial who holds any fascination for me. My learned friends, I hope you will prove that I am on the side of right.'

XIX

On 30 December, the last day of the year 1901, the judges finally announced the sentence: 'They have hardly opened the doors when a stream of people invade the courtroom. All the journalists and lawyers are present. The honourable Todeschini sits calmly in his seat and smokes a cigar. Lieutenant Trivulzio paces up and down the corridor.

'The court retired without even fixing an approximate time for the sentence to be announced. The obvious intention was to reduce the crowd. But the public resists this and, as usual, throngs the courtroom as well as the courtyard and the stairs.

'It's one o'clock when the court finally opens. There is an almost religious silence in the courtroom. Everyone is waiting in trepidation. President Pellegrini slowly reads the sentence. It upholds the charge of twofold libel by the honourable Todeschini and sentences him to 23 months' imprisonment, a fine of 1,458 lire, and payment to the public prosecutor of 3,000 lire for the expenses of setting up, damages and court costs. He orders the sentence to be published in the following newspapers: *Verona del Popolo*, *Corriere della Sera* and *Tribuna*.

'During the reading Todeschini stands, his face serious, turned towards his lawyers. When the President reads out "23 months" he looks momentarily disturbed, but recovers immediately and says quietly to his colleagues, "I'm going to hit the headlines!".

'Outside, the crowd fills the courtyard of the Palace of Justice. When the counsel for the defence comes out, it bursts into huge applause. It shouts out "Long Live Mario Todeschini, down with the Mafia!"

'The shouting mass then pours down the street into Via Quattro Spade where the typesetters for *Verona del Popolo* are located. They know that here they will find the honourable Todeschini. They go up the street shouting "Long live Todeschini!" Someone very loudly asks him to come out. After a great deal of insistence, Todeschini appears at the window and says a few words of thanks.

'The crowd then goes to Via San Egidio where the editorial

offices of *L'Arena* are situated and where, as a preventative measure, they have deployed a large force of civil and military police.'

Later on, the Stop Press column of *Il Gazzettino* read: 'Verona, 31 December 1901, 10.40 p.m. Last night approximately 2,000 railway workers, their ranks swollen by a number of other demonstrators, proceeded *en masse* from Porta Vescovo towards Via 20 Settembre, singing workers' songs and shouting "Down with the Mafia!"

'They reached Via Leoni without incident. Here they met up with a huge army of police. A police officer asked them to disperse. The demonstrators took no notice. Three blasts were blown on a trumpet and the demonstrators melted away. But they regrouped in Via Cappello in front of the Regina Margherita Hotel to cheer the honourable Todeschini. Another three blasts sounded and they began to make random arrests.

'There was an enormous panic and a general stampede. Todeschini, who had come out of the hotel, stood in the middle of the crowd and gave advice on how to disperse the crowd successfully.

'Fifteen people were arrested but on the orders of police officer Dallari they were released half an hour later.

'The city remains in a state of mild disturbance: patrols of police and military police march up and down the streets.

'We have been informed that Lieutenant Trivulzio left yesterday for Bassano.

'The grounds for the sentence will be published in fifteen days' time.'

The newspapers' comments were:

Verona del Popolo: Today the court sought justice, but instead destroyed it.

La Tribuna: Todeschini has been convicted because he wanted, by means of Trivulzio, to strike a blow at the army and its honour. In punishing Todeschini it is evident that the court was determined to destroy the efforts of the socialist party to besmirch an innocent person for political reasons. We welcome the sentence both for the sake of the army and Trivulzio.

Il Giornale d'Italia: The sentence justly condemns a man who wanted to vent an unjustifiable hatred against the army – a feeling of hatred which runs absolutely contrary to national feeling – by setting himself up as a judge of an officer in that army. It also completely vindicates the officer who, although he may have acted irresponsibly, has long since paid dearly for his irresponsibility. In any event the socialists have no right to condemn such irresponsibility, as they themselves practise free love.

Fanfulla: We applaud a sentence that we believe is a fair and decisive one. We applaud the magistrates for not allowing themselves to be influenced by the anti-militarist spirit of Todeschini's lawyers.

L'Arena: We have always believed that the campaign against Trivulzio was a case of moral and social insanity. For months we have suffered from poisons emanating from swamps infected with Red fever, where packs of howling dogs raged to tear the army limb from limb. . . .

L'Adige: We have nothing but praise for the sentence. We shall reserve our comments until after we have read the grounds for it.

La Provincia (in Padua): A thank-you to the magistrates of Verona, who knew how to vanquish whirlwinds of passion and sectarian hatreds. A thank-you to Trivulzio's lawyers, who have carried out their work in court not only with wisdom, but with a heartfelt patriotism.

Corriere della Sera: It is fortunate that in this trial, which has so disturbed the peace of a city as civilized as Verona, the magistrates passing sentence were extremely well known, either because they were born and bred in the city, or because in the long practice of their profession they came to be famous for their independence of spirit and their love of justice. . . . Lieutenant Trivulzio, with laudable discretion, left Verona as soon as he heard the sentence. The Commander of the Alpini regiment has taken the precaution of cutting short his soldiers' usual leave in order not to provoke those fanatics who might seize these poor young men and insult them by calling them 'butchers'.

No one remembered Isolina. The only newspaper that mentioned her was *La Liberta* in Padua, which wrote: 'All this unfortunately has not helped the main objective, which was to shed light on the murder of Isolina Canuti.'

PART FOUR

The Sentence

I

The long sentence was published punctually, fifteen days later. 'The court of Verona,' it read, 'second section, comprising Signor Pellegrini, Lawyer Carlo, High Officer President Arfini, Lawyer Fermo, Judge Ceccato, Lawyer Giulio on behalf of His Majesty Vittorio Emanuele III, King of Italy, with God's grace and the nation's will, pronounces the following sentence on Mario Filippo Todeschini, son of Natale Todeschini, aged 37, born and resident in Verona, Member of Parliament, who was charged with libel in the various articles he wrote . . . etc.'

In very few words the judges destroyed the evidence against Trivulzio even more quickly than the lawyers for the prosecution did, by taking everything that the lieutenant said as the truth. For example: 'In examining the results of these long proceedings, we must make our principal task in the above-mentioned trial, a study of the plaintiff's statements, in order to ascertain if they could even remotely provide grounds for serious attack by his opponent. And we can only answer that this is not the case, because Trivulzio has related all the circumstances of his relationship with Isolina Canuti in such a way as to justify completely the legal proceedings he set in motion. He confesses, in fact, that his relationship with Isolina Canuti began on the 27th of October when he was ordered under house-arrest. He denies that he ever went outside the house with her, admitting that he met her twice on the street . . . this is a statement that was never effectively denied during the trial. . . .'

As far as the powder is concerned, the judges do not think that Clelia Canuti would have lied, but that 'she may have been mistaken'. In fact, no one ever did deny what Clelia had to say, nor did they bring proceedings against her. 'But', the sentence continued, 'how can we attribute sound judgement to a girl who sided with her sister and said she had no other lovers at a time when it is a known fact that Isolina had had other relationships previously?'

Regarding Carlini, who gave evidence that he had found out about Trivulzio's request for an abortion from De Mori, the judges said that he was 'not credible because he talks about things other people have told him that he in turn reports to yet another person, so that in the judges' that opinion it is impossible for his various statements to be believed. In addition, the person who originally gave him information is an unreliable source, for reasons we shall go into later.'

The 'person who originally gave him information' was Maria Policante. When they talked about her, the judges' arguments became so convoluted as to be incomprehensible. 'Policante', they wrote, 'is perhaps the only person to accuse Trivulzio directly of doing things which *Verona del Popolo* also dared to say he did. However, we must bear in mind what the plaintiff himself says about her, which is that he explicitly and categorically states that everything she says is lies. In the judges' opinion, there is absolutely no reason to believe that Trivulzio's evidence is any less credible than that of any other witness in this trial.'

So in brief, when Trivulzio defended himself against various accusations, what he said was taken to be as valid as the statements of people who simply reported facts.

'The judges have no grounds for disbelieving Policante's evidence' they continued, perhaps realizing the absurdity of the preceding statement, 'but there is considerable room to believe that her whole testimony is a series of skilful manoeuvres in which she says only what she wants to say and nothing else.'

'We cannot exclude the possibility that Trivulzio might also be omitting things which he prefers not to tell us. At the same time, however, we would have to be quite certain that they were said deliberately and that he intended them to have certain consequences.' This last comment concerns the fact that Trivulzio never denied advising Isolina to go to Milan for an abortion.

In conclusion, said the judges, what the witnesses say 'are just so many words, and all of them lead us back to Policante's story; but against them we have Trivulzio's version of the facts, which never changes a single syllable in the telling and re-telling'.

And what about Cacciatori, the former chief constable who was the first to declare Trivulzio's guilt and have him arrested? 'We need to divide the chief constable's statements', said the judges, 'into those that refer to specific facts, and those that are his own convictions, and although we believe him to be impartial yet we are not wholly certain that his convictions are valid.' This is the height of Byzantine rhetoric. It is as if they were patting him on the back and saying what a fundamentally good man he was, but at the same time arguing that what he said did not carry any weight because he was an impressionable person.

As for Nimini, another important witness, 'To speak plainly, he knows nothing about what happened at firsthand, but has regurgitated the same descriptions of events that have been magnified out of all proportion by the public's curiosity. This has resulted in a trial that has become difficult to keep within certain limits.'

And Sitara: 'He said that until a few days after the 15th of September 1899, he took no notice of what Isolina told him about her condition; that he did not know if the relationship was still continuing; and that he knew nothing about either the midwife or the powder. He also said that he had never seen any other officers at the Canutis' house, nor did he ever see Policante talking to Trivulzio. Without wasting any more of our time, we want to say that we consider his statements to be completely lacking in the details that the witnesses above took pains to emphasize. . . .

'Sitara denies saying that he threw a bag containing a dog's carcass into the Adige, and admits that his master did own three bags used for military excursions. When these were shown to him at the preliminary investigation, he recognized two of them, but not the third. He absolutely denies that he threw the bags into the river. And we have no reason not to believe him. . . .'

These judges had an enormous talent for saying a great deal without saying anything, for telling a story with no content, for making a judgment without taking a stand. The tone of high moral indignation that they adopted makes them sound rather ridiculous.

When they came to discuss Isolina's morality, however, witnesses suddenly became people who were to be believed, rather than disbelieved. 'The witness Lucia Gemma says that after Trivulzio's arrest the neighbours were all on his side because Isolina used to have so many lovers. . . . The witness Sterza gives evidence that he believed Isolina to be a wicked girl. The witness Maria Di Maggio states that she heard from Clelia that apart from Trivulzio, Isolina had various other lovers and she also gave the circumstances that a certain Tommasoni had told her. They refer specifically to Isolina's relationship with a lieutenant in the Bersaglieri regiment. She learned from Clelia that he was a captain who had also made advances to Isolina and that he was possibly her lover too before Lieutenant Trivulzio went to live at the Canutis' house.

'The witness Bagnarelli also repeats the story about the lieutenant from the Bersaglieri regiment. He used to give Clelia his dog to look after while he amused himself with Isolina, who mistreated Clelia, even keeping her short of food.

'The witness Bernardini, an acquaintance of Isolina's, said that she had to tell her off because she was flirtatious. However, her scolding had little effect because she actually glimpsed Isolina and Policante completely naked in a room from her window. And Policante, who was a bad influence on Isolina, was pregnant at the time and then went to the midwife Friedman for an abortion. Once, in Isolina's house various officers kicked up a row, and she believes various things happened there, but this was all years before the crime took place. Isolina had also been told to get out by the landlord because she caused such scandals. . . .'

And again: 'The witness Preti Domenico repeats stories about the shameless behaviour of Policante and Isolina in the Canutis' house; the endless comings and goings of various men and women; the wild parties they had so that Canuti would sometimes yell at Isolina and Policante for their immodest behaviour. He also says that his cousin, who was the landlord of the house rented by the Canutis, promised – because people insisted on it – to evict them, but he had delayed doing this because he was scared of what Policante would do and he'd heard from her that Isolina was going anyway. . . .'

About Favaretti, they said 'We are unable to believe her testimony because she has said herself that it's very easy to make things up; and in addition she is an alcoholic.'

When they came to Isolina's pregnancy, the judges did not mince words. The baby's father was not Trivulzio because, they wrote, 'the witness Dallara testifies that she heard Isolina say something at the end of August that made her think she was pregnant; and that Isolina often talked loudly, so that once she heard her talking about how she had enjoyed herself with a captain. Dallara confirms that she could hear Isolina despite the fact that she was some way away. It was August; she was at an open window and she noticed that Isolina's stomach was obviously bulging. She remembers it was hot, because she also saw Isolina put a cape round her shoulders which was too heavy for that time of year.' In short, they recorded all the neighbourhood gossip and in addition, the gossip of neighbours who had nothing better to do than spy on Isolina. It is impossible to say whether these witnesses were so numerous because of their morality or because they were paid.

Probably these women were sincere in their fierce denigration of Isolina. The fact is that anyone who came to Isolina's defence was seen immediately as being 'a bad lot' and we know now how much a woman's reputation counted. The most striking proof of this is the fact that Trivulzio was able to save himself thanks to Isolina's bad name.

But let's get on to Trivulzio. Here the judges became magnanimous and sentimental. 'Described by all as being goodhearted, loyal, frank and conscientious in carrying out his military duties, despite his arrest which was simply a consequence of a quarrel with some youths – and no one is exactly sure whose fault it was. The officer is well known in the city for his moral uprightness and his sense of honour. Lieutenant

Ettore Martini confirms that Trivulzio was in the habit of going
to the Military Club every evening from six until eight-thirty
and that he believes utterly in the plaintiff's innocence. He
relates how on the evening before his arrest he slept for two
hours at the Officers' Club, then went in civilian clothes to the
Cavalchina, and then to the Ristori Theatre . . . the witness
Colonel Comi confirms the high regard in which Trivulzio was
held, says how much he admires the lieutenant's letter that was
published, tells how Todeschini had insulted the Alpini regiment as a whole and remembers how, following a bad report by
Captain Brugnoli, Trivulzio had dutifully reported the fact to
the captain. . . . And let's not forget the famous letter from
Trivulzio himself to his colonel, the letter that provoked so
much discussion because it was said that Trivulzio accused
himself in it . . . all the things that he wrote in it, for example
that he would kill himself if he knew he was guilty; that he
asked for his family's love; that he said how devoted he was to
his superior, the colonel; all these things are more than enough
to convince anyone that he was writing in the only way he
could, that is, declaring his innocence without paying too much
attention to the expressions he used to articulate a resentment
at being accused of such a crime. . . .'

On Gobbi and his extremely serious evidence: 'Isotta denies
that he ever said the things that were attributed to him. He
explains about the business of the fork – he was simply referring to current gossip. No matter what Gobbi and Manzoni say,
it was a rumour going around town at the time. . . .' So they
believe Isotta rather than Gobbi because they argue that as he
was the landlord of an inn whose reputation had been damaged
by gossip, it would have been illogical for him to support the
gossip with an actual account of what happened.

Gobbi's words were described as 'rumours' and 'fantastic
inventions'. Isotta would not have said things that could harm
himself. It was true that he had complained to Gobbi, but
that was only because his business at the inn had been going
badly ever since the rumour started going around town that
Isolina really had been killed there.

Carezzato's statements that he saw the windows lit up and

heard Isotta complaining about the officers were inexplicably described as being 'imprecise and ambiguous'.

'The witness Graziani relates how orgies were held at the Chiodo, that girls were given aphrodisiacs by unscrupulous soldiers, but all that was hearsay, not concrete fact . . . in addition, he repeats the story about what Sitara was doing at Selva di Progno (his confessing that he carried some sacks under orders from the 'three masters'). But as Sitara denies everything he is supposed to have said, we must keep to what he asserts.' For the judges, there was no difference between one statement and another, so they washed their hands of it all, because one excluded the other.

As for Benedetto Poli, who 'related how his daughter was poisoned in hospital', they said he was an unreliable witness because of the conflicting statements he made before the judges. And so the most mysterious and sinister event in the whole business was simply wiped out in a few words.

And the experts? The judges admitted that the experts Fagiolo and Pisa disagreed on the stage of Isolina's pregnancy at the time of her death. Fagiolo talked about the second month, while Pisa thought she was in her first month. But Professor Bonuzzi's authority overrode them both. And since Professor Bonuzzi established that the pregnancy was certainly six months, probably even seven, 'and in his role as expert confirms the above even admitting that the colostrum in the breasts is not in itself the only certain evidence of pregnancy . . .' the judges preferred to take his expertise into account. . . .

Finally, they made their conclusions, hypocritical in their tone of regret: 'Although the Court may be upset by what we have to say because we are commenting on someone whose life came to a miserable end, nevertheless the demands of Justice must be superior to any sentiment other than a desire for Truth. . . . We must uphold the unanimous opinion of the witnesses on Isolina's wild life, her various relationships, which some people believed made her a carrier of syphilis, the scandals she caused the neighbourhood, her shamelessness, and her immodest way of life, which more than one witness said was instigated by Policante.

'We also know, and this is indisputably to Trivulzio's credit, that he quickly informed the authorities when the suspicion arose that the remains found in the Adige might be Isolina's. It is also clear that we should attach no importance to the events that have been described concerning Sitara, Favaretti and Olivieri. These events, described in various conflicting ways, do not show in any way at all that Trivulzio was even remotely involved in this horrible affair which continues to be a complete and utter mystery. . . .

'We must also take into account that all Trivulzio's superiors and colleagues have spoken extremely highly of him. . . .

'In conclusion, since expert opinion states explicitly that the remains found in the Adige were those of a woman whose stage of pregnancy pre-dated the time when Trivulzio had a relationship with Isolina . . . it therefore follows that, given that those remains were unfortunately hers, the said lieutenant could not be considered responsible for the pregnancy. . . .

'In consequence, the Court finds the honourable Mario Filippo Todeschini guilty of continuous libel in the press against Carlo Trivulzio and sentences him to 23 months' and 10 days' imprisonment and a fine of 1,458 lire. It also orders him to pay court costs, to publish the sentence in his newspaper and to pay damages in compensation.'

And so Todeschini's trial concluded with a sentence that seems farcical because it was so obviously one-sided. You can read between the lines that they were saying Isolina got what she asked for. If her loose behaviour caused her tragic end, then so much the worse for her. On the other hand, as one newspaper wrote, Lieutenant Trivulzio had suffered for a long time and paid for his 'immorality', which the socialists were in no position to criticize since they themselves practised 'free love'. It's almost as if they were saying that murder was a natural part of free love!

However, they did make it clear in the sentence that they considered Trivulzio's morals to be wanting; that they might even have thought him irresponsible; but what, finally, did the life of a girl from a poor, obscure family count for, when opposed to the honour of the army? And it was that which finally triumphed, with all the strength of an ideology that gives expression to a country's ideal.